## "It's too

She looked at him, confused. "What are you saying, Zach?"

"I'm saying you can't go into the cave. Not after what happened yesterday."

Instantly her face changed. Her eyes went from trust to surprise, hurt, then fury. "The hell I'm not. I'm in charge of this project and you've been trying to take it away from me from the beginning. I...I can't trust you, can I?"

She spit the words at him, her angry eyes shimmering with unshed tears. This was what he needed to happen, to get her so mad she wouldn't speak to him. As much as he remembered making love to her, holding her, making her writhe under him, he couldn't give in. He had to keep her out of the cave.

As she turned away, the boulder where she'd been standing suddenly exploded, shards of rock hurtling through the air. Maxine pivoted toward the sound, obviously not realizing what it was.

"Get down!" Zach didn't have time to explain. He simply tackled her from behind. "Someone's shooting at us."

# KAY THOMAS

# BULLETPROOF TEXAS

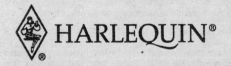

**HARLEQUIN®**

TORONTO • NEW YORK • LONDON
AMSTERDAM • PARIS • SYDNEY • HAMBURG
STOCKHOLM • ATHENS • TOKYO • MILAN • MADRID
PRAGUE • WARSAW • BUDAPEST • AUCKLAND

For Momma, who always listens, and for Te-Daddy,
who tells me I can do whatever I set my mind to.
You never stopped believing this was possible.

Recycling programs
for this product may
not exist in your area.

ISBN-13: 978-0-373-69397-9
ISBN-10:    0-373-69397-4

BULLETPROOF TEXAS

Copyright © 2009 by Kay Thomas

www.eHarlequin.com

**Printed in U.S.A.**

## ABOUT THE AUTHOR

Having grown up in the heart of the Mississippi Delta, Kay Thomas considers herself a "recovering" Southern belle. She attended Vanderbilt and graduated from Mississippi State University, with a degree in educational psychology and an emphasis in English. Along the way to publication, she taught high school, worked in an advertising specialty agency, and had a very brief stint in a lingerie store.

Kay met her husband in Dallas when they sat next to each other in a restaurant. Seven weeks later they were engaged. Twenty years later she claims the moral of that story is: "When in Texas look the guy over before you sit next to him, because you may be eating dinner with him the rest of your life!" Today she still lives in Dallas with her Texan, their two children and a shockingly spoiled Boston Terrier named Jack.

Kay is thrilled to be writing for Harlequin Intrigue and would love to hear from her readers. Visit her at her Web site, www.kaythomas.net, or drop her a line at P.O. Box 837321 Richardson, TX 75083.

### Books by Kay Thomas

HARLEQUIN INTRIGUE
1112—BETTER THAN BULLETPROOF
1130—BULLETPROOF TEXAS

# CAST OF CHARACTERS

**Dr. Max (Maxine) O'Neil**—She's a New York pharmaceutical research scientist working for Earth Pharm and searching for a cancer-eating bacteria hidden deep in Devil's Hollow. Can she overcome her deepest fears to find the cure to the deadliest scourge in history?

**Zach Douglas**—A former park ranger hired to help Max and her team find the bacteria, he blames all pharmaceutical companies for the recent death of his sister.

**Dr. Ralph Kirk**—Max's boss and surrogate father believes this project could be the best thing that's ever happened to his company, Earth Pharm, but only if the bacteria is kept top secret. How far is he willing to go to keep the discovery under wraps?

**Ellen Garrett**—She's a biochemistry graduate student who initially discovers the cancer-eating bacteria and part of the caving team hired to help the scientists from Earth Pharm. But can she be trusted to help retrieve the bacteria from deep inside the cave?

**Michael Lambert**—He is Zach's best friend and a member of the caving team. Can he keep Zach honest about why he wants inside Devil's Hollow while keeping everyone safe?

**Salvatore (Sal) Evans**—He is Max's right-hand man on the research team of scientists from Earth Pharm. Is he truly her ally?

**Rodger Martin**—He is an Earth Pharm scientist and the equipment wrangler for the researchers. Is Earth Pharm the only company he works for?

**Carl Madden**—He's a reporter for *The Reddington County Herald* out to prove that the scientists from Earth Pharm are really after diamonds in Devil's Hollow. Will he uncover their real secret?

**Mrs. Mabry**—She's the innkeeper at the lodge in Whispering Pines National Forest. But is she all she seems?

**Sheriff Harris**—He is up for re-election and prone to bribery. Can he be trusted to investigate the crimes committed surrounding the research at Devil's Hollow?

# Prologue

Zach Douglas broke through the tunnel floor at five-thirty in the afternoon. "Hey, y'all, I think—" He broke off on a whisper, his mouth dry from dust and dehydration. He cleared his raw throat and shouted up to the others, "Hey, I think I found a weak spot here!"

Tired muscles and aching fingers were instantly forgotten as rock gave way to nothingness and a puff of stale air blew into his sweat-drenched face. The team had been digging in the sticky mud all day, but this was what he'd been hoping for for the past two months. What he'd been looking for the past three years. A shudder of wonder and excitement shimmied down his spine.

"You got something, Zach?" Ellen called to him from the surface as she slid down along the ropes to land beside him. Her headlamp cast an eerie glow in the small vertical chamber. The floor slanted at a thirty-degree angle at one end of the ten-by-ten stone enclosure. The tunnel bulged out in the middle, so the area felt much larger than it actually was.

"Omigod!" She slapped a muddy hand on his shoulder. The biochem student loved to dig as much as the rest of the guys. "Michael, Don! Get down here now. Zach's breaking through!"

Zach shook his head as two more figures scrambled down the various ropes, their headlamps reaching into the darkness like Hollywood searchlights. Everyone crowded together, euphoria and adrenaline thick in the air. They all examined the place where he'd felt the puff of breeze.

Zach hated to wipe the excited expressions off their dust-streaked faces, but someone had to be the adult. He felt like a kid on Christmas morning, but Don was the only official minor. Still, Zach had to be the responsible one. He was the park ranger.

"Guys, we can't all be down here while I do this. I haven't set a bolt anchor yet to clip myself in." He pointed to the small hole he'd made. "This whole floor could collapse if there's a cavern underneath."

Michael nodded. "You're right, we shouldn't even be standing here, but it's just so exciting. I've never been on a dig where someone broke through before."

"Me, neither," admitted Zach. He looked around at Ellen's and Don's disappointed faces, trying to come up with a way for everyone to share the moment while keeping safe at the same time. As the more experienced of the four, he knew that hanging out on top of a compromised cavern floor discussing who would sling the final shovel of rock was the height of stupidity.

"Okay, here's what's doing. Y'all are going back topside while I set some protection and break through. If this were Caving 101, we'd all be getting an F. I'm going to clip in and make a bigger opening. Then we'll figure out what we've got and how to go through together."

Don and Ellen nodded. Michael wrapped the rope around his waist on hip belay and the others clipped in with their Jumars and shimmied back up the nylon lines. "You're lucky to have such agreeable folks working on this," Michael murmured.

"Don't I know it," said Zach.

The entrance was a new find. In his wildest dreams, he'd been hoping for something like Lechuguilla Cave, in New Mexico. Don, Michael and he were in it for the exploring.

Ellen was here for the science and her final thesis at the University of Texas.

They were on private property and permission to dig had been easy to obtain. So far the project had been pretty much a bust. Back-breaking, sweat-producing work with nothing to show for their efforts but good times. Working together on Zach's off weekends, few and far between all winter and spring, now they were finally at the payoff.

After Michael's ascent, Zach set a bolt anchor, clipped in and began hacking away at the rock. Topside, he could hear everyone talking. A bizarre anomaly in the tunnel allowed sound to carry from directly overhead. He even heard his own cell phone ringing in his backpack, one hundred feet above.

Three more swipes with his crowbar and he had a basketball-size hole. The wind below sucked the pebbles, dirt and rock down inside like a giant vacuum so that he didn't even have to clear away the debris. There must be a good-size chamber underneath him to have that kind of suction. He kept working at the opening until it was large enough to slip his head and shoulders through.

Ellen, Don and Michael looked down at him, calling encouragement. But he barely heard them now, his heart pounding with excitement. His palms were slick with sweat.

He'd been hooked on caves since he was a kid and visited Carlsbad Caverns with his family. He'd loved everything about the underground rooms and majestic formations. Even when he and his sister had gotten separated from the main tour, he hadn't been frightened. He'd been fascinated.

Tammy. God, his twin would love this. Well, she wouldn't like the dirt part anymore, but she'd love the discovery part. He couldn't wait to make that call.

It took more than a little courage for him to put his head inside the gaping hole in the tunnel floor not knowing what was down there. Kind of like *Roman Holiday*. Tammy'd talked him into renting it at Blockbuster when she'd come to visit last month. Expanding his "chick flick" education, she'd said. They'd stuffed themselves with buttered popcorn and watched Gregory Peck and Audrey Hepburn putting their hands into a gargoyle's mouth.

Zach lay on his stomach with his head and shoulders sticking straight down into the hole. There was just enough clearance for him to squeeze through and still use his hands to pull himself back up and out. He felt the blood rush to his head as he slipped into the pit. Cool air blew against his face. His headlamp wasn't very bright, but wild, beautiful rock formations were clearly visible—gypsum crystal melting away into deep shadows of what must be a tremendous chamber. He flicked on the high-powered flashlight and his breath caught.

The cavern below was massive, at least three or four hundred feet long, by his estimate. He hung sixty feet in the air, upside down over the floor. His light didn't reach quite to the ends of the room. At the far edge of one wall was a huge pool and what appeared to be a waterfall.

Their new cave was obviously part of the Edwards Aquifer system, just as he'd suspected. The other end, or what he could see of it, contained immense calcite curtain formations and mountainous soda straws. A magical-looking fairyland. The fact that his were the first eyes to have ever seen the soaring walls and undulating flowstone made it that much more amazing.

He couldn't wait to get down on the cavern floor and examine everything up close. He raised his head out of the chasm with a silly grin on his face. It was like leaving another world.

"Guys, you won't believe this," he called up to the team, still feeling a little dizzy.

"Zach? Zach?" Michael, Don and Ellen were all calling down to him. Their voices were no longer excited; they were panicked.

"You've got to tell him," whispered Ellen.

"I don't want to." Michael sounded angry.

"Someone has to," insisted Ellen.

*What the hell?* They had no idea he could hear every word.

Don and Ellen peered down at him. Michael was now halfway down the rope without a belay.

"Are they sure?" Don whispered to Ellen. "I mean, they have positive ID on her?"

Zach's blood ran cold.

Michael landed at his feet. The light from the headlamp made him look washed-out and pale, an awful sadness in his eyes.

*No.* Whatever Michael had to say, Zach didn't want to hear this. Not here, not today.

"Zach, your phone kept ringing. I figured it must be an emergency so I answered. There's…there's been a murder."

Jesus. "Where? At the park?"

As a ranger he would be needed at the scene ASAP. Zach took a deep breath and waited for Michael to respond. His heart rate should have begun to return to normal, but it didn't. An uneasy feeling swept over him like a cold wind as he looked into Michael's face.

"So I've got to get back to the park station. My God, who was killed?"

Michael shook his head. "You don't understand. The murder wasn't here." That sadness in his eyes deepened as he reached out to put a hand on Zach's shoulder. "It happened in Dallas. The phone call was from your mother."

*No, no.* Zach felt the air leave his lungs, but Michael continued to speak.

"I'm so sorry, Zach. They found Tammy this afternoon in her apartment. Your sister was murdered."

# Chapter One

*Three months later*

Maxine O'Neil bounced in the passenger seat of the Jeep Grand Cherokee as the Texas landscape flashed by in the pouring rain. The boy—well, he was seventeen, she'd seen his Park ID—drove like a bat out of hell over the rugged terrain.

Her head almost hit the ceiling as her jean-clad butt left the seat. The windshield wipers scratched across the glass in harmony to Toby Keith blaring from the dashboard about loving him even though you might hate his politics.

How in the world had she ended up in Reddington, Texas?

The answer was simple. She'd walked in on her fiancé screwing his administrative assistant on the new office sofa. A "goodbye boff," the idiot had claimed in his smooth British accent, once he'd gotten his pants back up.

She hadn't cried. She'd just stood there in shock for a moment, the oddest thoughts popping into her head. Like did the vacation insurance she'd purchased for their upcoming cruise cover this eventuality?

Death in the immediate family. Serious illness. Car accident on the way to the port.

Catching your fiancé doing his secretary the day of departure? Boffing insurance. Probably not covered by Caribbean Cruise Lines.

Forty-five minutes later she sat on another sofa with a strong cup of her mentor's Darjeeling tea in hand—her cruise and engagement now a thing of the past.

"He did what?" shouted Kirk, jumping up from behind his desk and nearly overturning his own ever-present cup of tea. "On that lovely new sofa you helped him pick out? Good God, they'll ruin the upholstery."

Max stifled a sad giggle. Traitorous moisture seeped behind her lashes.

"That effing idiot," growled Kirk in his Scottish brogue, gray hair sticking out in all directions. He looked like a red-faced, overweight Einstein. "What the hell was he thinking?"

Max swallowed before she answered. "Oh, he explained all that. He told me he wasn't thinking. He was reacting—to Marcie—with his penis."

"Horseshit."

She did laugh then. Because it was so true. This was all horseshit. The picture of Robert scrambling to pull up his boxers and slacks as he explained his "goodbye boff," or "the GB" as it would forever be labeled in her head, while Marcie smirked in the background.

They'd given that twit a Coach handbag for Christmas. Robert always insisted on spectacular gifts for his "support staff." Jesus.

Max shook her head at the hideous memory and dug in her purse for her Relpax tablets. The neurologist had said she should take them as soon as she felt a headache coming on. Not to wait.

Lord, if she'd known what today had held, she'd have taken two before she got out of bed. She took her medicine with the hot tea and wished for a double shot of tequila, but it was only ten-thirty in the morning.

"So did you kick him in the balls?" Her former college professor was rabid about his female employees knowing how to defend themselves.

"No, I'm afraid I didn't. I acted like a girl."

He looked stricken. "Don't tell me you cried in front of that prick. You're thirty-two years old, for God's sake."

Oh, she adored this man. Ralph Kirk held her accountable and loved her like the daughter he'd lost. The one male figure in her life she didn't have to pretend to or put on any kind of front with.

"No. No. I just stood there like a duck in thunder. I couldn't figure out what to do. Then Marcie piped up about how they'd been seeing each other for several months and I lost it."

"What did you do?"

"I threw a paperweight at him."

Kirk gave an inelegant snort.

"I'm pretty sure it's the one you gave him last year. I think I must have clipped him. He didn't have his pants up yet. He was still trying to 'talk me down.'"

Kirk smiled his toothy grin and began to cackle like a rooster on crack.

She shook her head. "Don't laugh too hard. You're gonna hear about this, I'm sure."

"I just hope I do."

"But, Ralph, he could sue you. And, of course, me. I mean, he was bleeding when I left. Besides that he's the most litigious man I know."

"Hell, woman." Kirk shrugged. "Let him fuss. He was balling another Earth Pharm employee in my offices on my nickel. He'll most likely be sued for sexual harassment himself before it's over."

"No." Max closed her eyes, not because of the crudity of the terms, but because of the mess this was shaping up to be.

Kirk nodded. "Max, he'll lose his job. The company shrink can't screw his secretary on company time and get away with it. Not to mention cheat on his fiancée, the VP of Development, and not expect consequences."

Mentally Max cringed. The publicity and the pity of her fellow coworkers. The thought of all the fallout to come ratcheted her headache up a notch.

"But even my lawyers will say you've got to get out of here while we deal with all this. You don't want to be around when we fire this idiot."

"No, I certainly don't." She struggled not to whine. "You know we'd been planning to go on a cruise. Hell, my bags are in the lobby." She took a deep sip of tea and swallowed hard. "I agree I've got to get away for a while. I needed a break before all this happened. I just… I don't know if I can face the Caribbean by myself right now."

"Darlin', you don't want to go on a cruise alone, although I agree you do need a change of scene. You've been working nonstop upstairs in the lab. And it just so happens I have the ideal place for you. I'd wanted to ask you about it before—in fact, you were my first choice—but I knew you were taking a vacation. However, now that your plans have changed, this is perfect."

"What's perfect?" She took another slug of tea and imagined it to be Patrón Silver.

"It's called Devil's Hollow."

"That sounds like the remake of a bad Halloween movie. What's Devil's Hollow?"

"Cute." He pulled out a file folder as he spoke. "It's a newly discovered aquifer cave near Reddington, Texas. A friend of mine in Austin teaches at UT. One of his students is a spelunker, caver—whatever they call themselves. She isolated bacteria in a new cavern pool with some rather fascinating properties and used the special microbes for her thesis project. My friend thought I might be interested."

"Really." Max was still feeling sorry for herself and only halfway listening.

"I was all set to go down myself and take a look at things with Sal Evans and a small research team, but now that you're available…" He left the idea hanging. "You could go in my stead. I have the field lab already in place and Sal left this morning with the techs. I just need someone to oversee the project."

"Hmm." She slumped into Kirk's luxurious leather sofa,

trying to wipe out the memory of Robert and his bimbo on the couch three floors below. A new bacteria didn't sound very promising. But she asked the prerequisite question anyway because one, this was Ralph and he was trying very hard to help her take her mind off the abysmal state of her personal life. And two, the incident in Robert's office could become a professional problem—courtesy of her quick temper and sure aim with a crystal paperweight.

"What's so special about these bacteria?" She sipped her Darjeeling.

"They eat cancer cells."

Max bobbled her teacup, rattling the Wedgwood cup and saucer. "What?"

"The bacteria eat cancerous tissue and leave healthy tissue behind."

Her eyes widened and she sat up straighter on the sofa, Robert and his tart forgotten. "Are you sure?"

He nodded, a small smile playing about his face as he nonchalantly opened the file on his cluttered desk.

"Good Lord. That's unbelievable." She swallowed. "Can it be reproduced? Does anyone else know about it? Have you seen it yet? Do you know what this means?"

He raised an eyebrow and stared at her. "To answer your questions, I don't know, I don't know, no and yes. If the bacteria can be cultured outside the cave on a large scale, I've got a pretty good idea we'll be turning the world of cancer research upside down."

He stood and walked around the captain's desk to put a hand on her shoulder. "Now breathe, darlin'."

Max realized she was looking at him with a wild-eyed expression and that she hadn't taken one sip of oxygen or tea since he'd started talking about cancer-eating microbes.

"Are you interested?"

She took a gulp of air, huffed a laugh and nodded her head vigorously. "Hell, yes, I'm interested. This is amazing."

"Indeed it is." He poured himself more tea. "Now there is one catch, and for you, dear, it's a pretty big one. This field research and lab will all be inside Devil's Hollow."

"Uh-huh." She picked up her cup automatically as he motioned to refill it.

"That's a cave, Max."

"Right." She didn't really hear him, so lost in the possibilities of what the research could mean for Earth Pharm.

He leaned down, in her face, holding the teapot in one hand and gesturing with another. "A cave. You hear me, girl? A dark, closed-in, claustrophobia-producing cave. Can you handle that?"

Max stared at him, finally absorbing the information. A cave. *Damn.* Her worst nightmare.

She said the first thing that came to mind. The honest answer. "I'm not sure, but I'll die if I don't get to try this."

He looked at her and smiled sadly, none of the teasing or slyness in his eyes now. "Yes, I know, but there's no shame in not being able to do this if you can't. None at all. Your mother would understand. She wouldn't want you to—"

"Stop it, please." Max held up her hand; she'd just gotten over being weepy. "I'll be fine or I'll tell you if I'm not. I'd never jeopardize a project like this. You know that. And I'll take Tim Ryan with me. If I can't handle the lab work inside the cave for any reason, he can gather the samples and I can analyze the data topside. I trust his work implicitly."

He nodded. "Fair enough."

"Tell me everything."

"The cave is on private farmland adjoining Whispering Pines National Forest, so we've leased the farm for the next six weeks. If this bacteria is for real, we'll negotiate to purchase."

"Has it remained closed since the initial discovery?"

Kirk shrugged. "That's anyone's guess. This grad student could have been throwing keg parties there for all I know. It's why I wanted to get someone on-site as soon as possible. From now on no one goes in or out unless an Earth Pharm representative says they do. That's a lease stipulation."

"It's a good thing you knew this professor at UT or our bacteria could just as easily have ended up in some competitor's lap, huh?"

"Don't even think that out loud, darlin'. Until we have solid lab results and are certain that the bacteria can be cultured and reproduced outside the cave, no one outside Earth Pharm can know about the project."

Max leaned forward. "I'm not sure I understand."

"We don't own the property or the mineral rights yet. The owner is hesitant to agree to my terms." Kirk sipped his tea. "But he will. The short-term lease buys us time. But the true nature of this project must remain top-secret or it could get stolen right out from under us. As a cover story, we're going to call it mineral research for women's makeup."

"Women's makeup?"

"That's big business and as far from cancer research as you can get. Earth Pharm is branching out and expanding its markets, so this makes sense. It'll also make your cover easier to sell. You'll still be gathering samples from the pond. The grad student and her professor have signed nondisclosure agreements about what the samples are really for."

Max nodded. "Sounds like a plan."

They spent the rest of the morning and early afternoon mapping out her approach for the research. Max's lab would have been cutting back hours and staff while she was out of town anyway. That's why Sal and some of her techs were already en route to Devil's Hollow. Now Max would just be taking Kirk's place overseeing the project.

She was entirely convinced that her boss was the Pied Piper. She'd gone to his office to request an extended leave of absence and come out in charge of the biggest plum in the company. Devil's Hollow.

The project was a total fluke. Bacteria that ate only cancer cells and left healthy tissue behind. Amazing.

So many lives could be saved. So many that could have *been* saved. Their findings had the chance to revolutionize cancer research and make Earth Pharm the brightest star in the pharmaceutical world. Hell, the brightest in the Fortune 500.

Max stared out the window at the swiftly passing trees. This opportunity at Devil's Hollow was a godsend. The chance of a lifetime. And thanks to Kirk, she wouldn't have to think about the fiasco with Robert until she was good and ready.

The Jeep hit a large pothole and a migraine fluttered to life in the back of her head. She grimaced, reaching into her backpack for the medication that had been keeping the headaches mostly at bay for three months now. One more month wouldn't hurt. Then she'd be back to her old life and she could figure out what she needed to make it work. Not that she'd ever trust a man again—but maybe a sabbatical, a cruise or a wild fling would be just the thing for her flagging confidence. For now she just wanted inside that cave.

"Ma'am?"

The boy-child next to her had spoken. "We're almost to the Lodge."

"Oh, I thought we would stop by the cave first."

Looking at her designer sandals and capri pants, he frowned. Inwardly, she cursed Robert. He had locked her out of her own apartment the night of "the GB," the ass.

She'd spent last night in a hotel with her vacation clothes. There'd been no time to change or repack once she got back into her loft. Robert had moved out with all of his things and many of hers…including her entire Toby mug collection.

She still couldn't believe he'd taken the antique Royal Doulton jugs. The man didn't even have a cabinet to keep them in. He couldn't possibly care about such things.

He'd always made fun of her when she'd bought one of the unique face mugs at a flea market or hobby shop. She wouldn't be surprised if he'd tossed the whole box in the first Dumpster he passed walking out of their apartment. He'd taken them only to hurt her.

She clenched her fists as the anger rekindled and steam rolled out of her ears over this final insult. She was going to have to completely start over to rebuild the collection. Probably even have to learn to use eBay.

This morning she'd barely had time to get into the loft, throw some field clothes in a duffel bag and get to the airport for her flight. There hadn't been time to change.

The young chauffeur's eyes lingered longer than necessary on her white linen shirt before he looked away. She glanced down. One of the buttons had worked itself loose. That "minimizer" bra didn't appear to be doing the job she'd paid sixty-eight bucks for at Victoria's Secret. She reached up and rebuttoned the blouse.

The boy blushed and stammered, "Ah, you want to change first and get settled in? Zach Douglas said no one goes in or out unless he's there the first time."

"Oh, I was under the impress—" She stopped herself.

*Who the hell was Zach Douglas?* The cave was leased to Earth Pharm for the next six weeks. She was in charge of who went in and out.

Max decided to try the more-flies-with-honey version of her personality first. She'd been in Texas only six hours but had figured out that much. "Can't we just take a peek?"

She tried hard not to sound like a whiner. But she'd endured an interminable plane ride, a puddle jumper in a bailing wire-type operation, and now this Jeep ride that was going to have her ass bruised for a week. Not to mention a bra that was cutting her circulation off and not doing diddly. She wanted to see that cave now.

"No, ma'am. Zach wouldn't like it." He shook his head. "It's awfully muddy and you really need the proper clothing. He's there right now at the cavern setting things up for your team tomorrow. Getting into the cavern is not just strolling down a paved sidewalk. And with all this rain it's dicey. You have to be lowered on ropes through the entrance or rappel down."

He struggled to keep his eyes on her face, but failed miserably. "Um, do you rappel, ma'am?"

*Sure, right after I hang glide into the office every morning.* Her jaw creaked as she clamped down on the instinctive smart-ass reply. At this rate she would never get rid of her migraines and would most likely need a chiropractor for TMJ issues before the project was over.

"No." She'd never so much as held a carabiner in her hand and she was beyond pissed. This Zach Douglas was at the cave and she wasn't allowed there?

The boy—what was his name? *Don*—looked at her shoes with what she suspected was a patronizing air.

"Mmm-hmm." He draped a hand across the steering wheel, glanced at her chest again and shook his head slightly. "I see. Uh, we'll go on to the Lodge then."

*Who was this boy?*

Her headache blossomed into a mushroom cloud of pain and suddenly she'd had it with all the "ma'ams" that made her feel as old as her aunt Ethel. Now she was being judged by a twelve-year-old and told she couldn't see what she was frickin' in charge of.

"Pull over."

"Ma'am?"

"I said pull the hell over." Max dug into her bag, searching for the Relpax and wishing for a glass of ice-cold Perrier to wash it down. Reaching up with one hand to switch off the country music, she located the single-dose packet of migraine medication, ripped it open and swallowed the tablet dry.

"Uh, yes, ma'am."

Her infant chauffeur watched with wide eyes. For a moment she thought he would swallow his Adam's apple. What, had he never seen someone take a pill before?

"Look, Don. I'm in charge of this little soiree and I want to see the damn caverns today. So take me there. I don't give a rip who thinks he's in charge. I've been traveling for twelve hours and I'm a little testy as you can see."

He murmured something under his breath that sounded suspiciously like "No shit."

But she barreled on. "So…you're going to take me to see Zach Douglas now. And I don't give a rat's ass where he is. Got it?"

Don audibly swallowed again and murmured, "Yes, ma'am."

He threw a doubtful glance her way and shook his head as they sped through a rock archway into Whispering Pines National Forest and muttered under his breath, "I'd pay money to see this."

As they bounced over more potholes from hell, Max leaned her head against the seat and closed her eyes, willing the medicine to work faster than was chemically possible. Insisting on coming to the cave was possibly a mistake. But there was no backing out now.

She certainly shouldn't have lost her temper. She'd regretted that as soon as it happened. But damn it, she wanted to see Devil's Hollow and she hated the thought of someone who looked to be half her age telling her what she could and couldn't do.

There'd been some confusion at the airport when Don had picked her up. It had a taken a while for them to find each other. She'd waited thirty minutes in baggage claim before he had figured out that she was Dr. Max O'Neil and not the overweight businessman viewing cyberporn on his laptop seated near her. Of course, she probably shouldn't have assumed Don was too young to have a driver's license and couldn't possibly have been her chauffeur, either.

Still no excuse to have lost her temper with the boy.

She kept her eyes shut and they rode on in silence until she couldn't stand herself.

"Uh, Don?"

"Yes, ma'am?"

They'd slowed a bit from their earlier breakneck speed. She'd already tried to get him to stop "ma'am-ing" her when they'd finally found each other at the airport. That didn't seem to be working. "I'm sorry I blew up at you."

She felt his eyes on her every now and then as he drove, even though her own eyes were closed and her head lay against the headrest. She'd never gotten used to it. Boys and men stared at her. For a long time, she'd tried to convince herself it was her height.

At five foot eleven and a half inches in her bare feet, Max was striking. But she knew Don's gaze had more to do with her other attributes. She wasn't vain, but Max looked more like a Hooter's Girl than a scientist. She'd done modeling jobs to work her way through college when she was an undergrad.

And hated everything about it.

Not her looks, just the fact that men didn't take her brains seriously until she'd proven herself or shown them she wasn't an airhead. As a consequence, she'd developed a hard-ass persona for the job. She knew how to turn it on and off. And unfortunately, she'd needed it "on" quite often in her male-dominated profession.

She didn't necessarily like herself this way. Her Southern-belle mother would be horrified, and at times Max fleetingly wondered if she had a multiple-personality disorder. But the shock factor of hearing an Amazon woman yell at him usually straightened boys like this one right up. Of course, she always felt the need to apologize later.

"S'okay, you've had a long day." Don broke in on her private pity party.

She finally opened her eyes to look at him. "Well, that's very generous of you. I think it was inexcusable on my part."

"Don't worry about it, Dr. O'Neil, really." He grinned then

turned back to the road. "I'm glad I'm getting to take you to the cave to meet Zach, really. I wouldn't miss this for the world."

"I don't understand."

"No, ma'am. But you will."

## Chapter Two

Zach stood under a ledge sheltering the entrance to Devil's Hollow and watched rain drip down the rock face. Beside him, Ellen bustled, arranging the ropes and preparing for their descent into the cavern.

"I'm so excited. This feels like Christmas morning. I still can't believe Professor Weatheridge knew Dr. Kirk at Earth Pharm."

"Right." Zach attempted to dredge up a smile. But her words brought back bitter memories of another day that had felt like Christmas at the cave for him.

He couldn't quite believe that it had come to this. Not anywhere near the same enthusiastic high as Ellen, he figured he was doing well enough not to bite the girl's head off for what she'd done. That the caverns had been leased to Earth Pharm for women's makeup research was just one more blow on top of so many others over the past twelve weeks. Of course it would be a pharmaceutical company.

*Jesus, Tammy.* The sudden stab of pain in his chest was so ragged and unexpected, he closed his eyes a moment. He still couldn't believe she was dead. He took a deep breath, but at least he didn't tear up. Ellen rattled on, oblivious.

"And now you're finally back here, too. I'm so glad we were able to get in touch with Dr. Kirk today directly. He was thrilled to hear that an experienced caver was available and willing to help Earth Pharm's people while they're on-site."

She lowered her voice in a conspirator's tone. "These scientists apparently don't know beans about caving. I was worried about handling all that myself with just Michael and Don."

Zach cringed inwardly. *Damn.* He was already starting to regret his snap decision. But when he'd heard the cave had been leased and this was the only way inside, he'd taken the opportunity offered. Ellen had been more than happy to hook him up with Earth Pharm and its new cosmetics research team.

Michael walked over and pulled more rope from the pack. Zach could clearly see two harnesses at the bottom of the bag. There were three generators to set up today plus the electrical, lights and battery packs to get down to the first staging area of the cave.

Ellen droned on about Earth Pharm and their environmental stance on production. Zach was practically biting his tongue when Michael sat back to study the harnesses for a moment. He shot Zach an apologetic glance as he zipped the pack shut. "Well, hell," he muttered.

"What is it?" she asked. Michael's mild expletive had stopped her cold. The man never cussed in front of her.

Zach watched in wondering detachment as his friend lied like a rug to the doctorate student. "I think I must've left the harnesses in my truck. Ellen, could you go get them for me back at the gate?"

She sighed, the long-suffering sound of one who will do what is asked, but wants those around to know she is put out. "Jeez, Mickey. You'd forget your head if it wasn't screwed on."

"I know, sweetheart. That's why we've got you here—to keep me straight. There are three harnesses in the backseat…in the locker." He flashed her a repentant grin. "I'm sorry."

Ellen stalked over to Zach and held out her hand for the keys. Her happy mood was somewhat deflated as she flounced off in the rain to his truck.

"What was that about?" asked Zach, once she was out of earshot.

"I figured you were tired of hearing her wax poetic about Earth Pharm, right?"

Zach's shoulders slumped and the false front he'd been wearing since his arrival yesterday melted away. Michael, thank God, always cut right past the crap.

"Yeah, you're right. All pharmaceutical companies are bastards as far as I'm concerned." He turned to complete a complicated knot on a carabiner.

"What's going on, Zach? You quit your park service job, you don't return phone calls or e-mails for weeks, then when you do finally show up you immediately hire out as a short-term caving guide. I'm confused."

Zach closed his eyes. Michael was right. He hadn't called anyone. He'd shut them all out after the funeral. But he wasn't sure he could talk about it yet. "What's confusing? It's good pay. You're here."

"I need the money," said Michael matter-of-factly. "But you don't. You had a good job waiting on you and you gave it up. Why?"

He wasn't going to say, "I just need more time." Because this was his best friend since high school he'd been ignoring. So he decided to tell the truth, even though he wasn't sure how he felt about it. He couldn't deal with one more disappointed person today.

"It's about Tammy's murder."

Michael zipped the duffel bags he'd been working with and leaned against the rock face behind him. "What about it?"

"She was mixed up in some kind of pharmaceutical company drug cover-up. It sounds crazy but a coworker of hers, Gina Rodgers, came to see me last week at my folks' house before I came back. She and her boyfriend told me the whole story."

"Our Tammy?"

"I know, hard to believe. She got caught up in that vaccine scandal involving the senator and PharmaVax."

"That thing I heard about on CNN?"

"Yeah. That *thing* that made the cover of *Newsweek*." Zach shook his head. "The hell of it is Tammy didn't know what she was getting into. She was just holding Gina's mail for her and they murdered her for it."

"My God. Talk about wrong place wrong time," said Michael.

Zach nodded miserably and took another deep breath. Maybe it would have been better to keep his mouth shut.

"So why are you doing this instead of working for the park service?" asked Michael.

Zach shrugged. "To take my mind off it. All I could think about during the funeral and closing her apartment was getting back here and losing myself in exploring Devil's Hollow for a while. I couldn't believe it when I got here and the place had been leased."

"So why are you helping them?" Michael asked again.

"I've just got to get inside that cave. Just to… I don't know. It's where I was right before this happened. What I've looked for my whole life. I want to explore it. Map it."

"And you think this is what you need to get over your sister's death?"

It would have been smarter to have never started this conversation. "Screw you, Michael. Nothing's going to get me over it. I know that. And I know this is probably not what I need. But it's what I want. And if the only way to get what I want is babysitting a bunch of overweight, overpaid scientists who've never set foot out of a laboratory, then so be it."

Michael didn't react; he merely raised a skeptical eyebrow.

Zach didn't care. At this moment, he had to get inside the cave. Something…anything to take his mind off how much losing Tammy made him ache. He was an ass for taking this out on his friend, but in his present state, he couldn't afford to care.

Jesus. Maybe Michael was right. He shouldn't be here.

In fact, working for someone new when he was so defensive and hostile was probably the last thing he needed to be doing from a career standpoint.

But there was no hope for it. He'd accepted the job this afternoon. And there was no other way to get into the cave. Dr. Max O'Neil and his team better at least be in shape and not some salad-dodging old men who didn't ever get out of their office chairs.

A honking horn interrupted his personal diatribe.

Zach's truck and then Don's rolled to a stop. Ellen hopped out. "Hey, I've got the harnesses, and Don brought the doctor up here."

Zach shook his head and went back to coiling rope. Great. The missing ingredient for his personal moment of enlightenment.

Michael spoke the obvious. "I thought the kid was going to get Dr. O'Neil and take him back to the Lod—" His voice broke off as Don's passenger door opened. "Whoa," he murmured. "What the hell is this?"

Zach looked up to see a statuesque redhead climb out of the Jeep and look up at the sheer cliff face and ledge.

More like *who* the hell was this? Zach thought. Dr. Max O'Neil was a man with a team of crusty scientists—at least that's what he'd been expecting.

This woman, worthy of a magazine spread, slid glasses down her perfect nose and perused the scene. She was taking it all in and Zach noticed a tiny furrow between her brows, like something was bothering her about what she was seeing. Raindrops spattered her shirt, making it transparent wherever they landed. He struggled not to stare.

She held out her hand and walked forward. "Hello, I'm Dr. Maxine O'Neil." Her voice was deep and hoarse. "Call me Max."

"Hi, I'm Ellen Garrett."

"Ah, so you're the woman who made this amazing discovery."

Ellen glanced nervously at Zach before answering. "Well, not the cave, just the pond."

"Yes, but I hear it's quite an amazing body of water."

"That may be," replied Ellen, "but the real explorer here is Zach."

Ellen looked hopefully at him, trying to please. He took about five seconds longer than usual before he stepped forward and took Dr. O'Neil's offered hand.

Ellen took care of the introductions. "Zach Douglas, Dr. Max O'Neil. Dr. O'Neil, this is Michael Lambert."

Everyone shook hands.

Max, short for Maxine... *Great.* "We weren't expecting to meet you here," said Zach carefully.

"I wasn't expecting to meet you at all, Mr. Douglas. I was told that I was in charge of Devil's Hollow."

*Okay.* There was a moment of measured silence as Zach met her eyes, digesting the message she'd delivered and registering the cold bucket of ice water she'd doused over their greeting. Obviously she was pissed that no one had told her he was here to help.

"Yes, ma'am. You are in charge. This afternoon your boss, Dr. Kirk, hired me to guide you and your team inside the caverns. The conditions can be somewhat treacherous. I believe the extra precautions are a good idea." He kept his voice steady and even.

In the past he'd been quite good at keeping cool in situations where others were losing it. That's what made him a good caver and guide. But right now his emotions were in a place they'd never been before in all his thirty-five years.

Max O'Neil studied him, actually had to look up at him in the sporadic, spitting rain. She was tall, but he was six foot five. "I see. Well, I'd like to get inside the cave this afternoon just to see what we are up against. I need to make an initial report."

The woman was tenacious; he'd give her that. Zach leaned back against the rock face behind him, much like the stance Michael had taken earlier.

"That won't be possible, Dr. O'Neil. We're not ready. You'd have to rappel down into the entrance and conditions are slick from this weather. It's not a good idea."

She frowned. The wrinkle between her brows creased further. "You just said I'm in charge."

Michael cleared his throat in what might have been a cover for a laugh. Mentally Zach took a deep breath and attempted to radiate a calm, zenlike demeanor. Inwardly he seethed. This woman pushed his buttons in every negative way possible.

"That's right. And I was hired to keep you and your team safe. I understand none of you has much experience in caves."

He met her eyes. There was something there. A shudder, a shiver. He wasn't sure, but he didn't stop to explore it. He'd press that later if he had to.

She looked at the multiple duffels of equipment under the ledge. "Well, if you don't feel you're up to the job, I'm sure Kirk can hire someone else."

Zach let the bitchy comment lie there for a moment. The weight of the words seemed to work on her before an audience. He could tell by the way she held herself. He would stay above it all, no matter what she said. He was bigger than that, but also very distracted by the wet-T-shirt-contest entry she was quickly becoming. "Right now, the cave's not safe and you're not dressed for a walk on the wild side, so to speak."

She glanced down at her damp linen top and sighed as she buttoned the top closure. When she looked back up at Zach her eyes were fierce. "They're just breasts, Mr. Douglas, and they don't preclude me from having a brain."

"Of course not. But it would be better to wait until tomorrow when you're well rested and we have all the equipment ready." He kept his voice low and even. "You can even have dry clothes."

She didn't even crack a smile at his attempted humor. "I have all my clothes here." She pointed to the Jeep. "I can change in five minutes. I need to see the cave today and get that initial report out to *our* boss."

For a moment Zach couldn't decide if she sounded like a spoiled child or a woman trying to convince herself of something. And suddenly, he'd had enough of Dr. Max O'Neil who should have been an overweight middle-aged man, but instead was a hot thirty-something woman. He also didn't think he could handle her stripping down right here in the great outdoors. No more kid gloves. She wanted to play hardball. He'd oblige.

"Well, we don't always get what we want, do we, Dr. O'Neil? Suck it up. Your cosmetics report will have to wait a few hours. We'll be ready for you and your team tomorrow morning at eight."

Behind him Ellen was having apoplexy, but he couldn't care less.

"And if I insist on going in today?"

"I quit right now and you can find your own way into Devil's Hollow. Good luck with that."

He turned to walk away and gathered the gear as Ellen gasped.

"Wait, Mr. Douglas." A cool hand touched his arm. Zach held his breath and faced the woman who was rapidly becoming his worst nightmare.

Her auburn hair was piled in some kind of clip on top of her head, but the rain had misted it all. Curly strands had come loose and now clung to her cheeks and forehead, accenting piercing blue eyes. He hadn't been close enough before to notice that she had creamy skin, a tiny smattering of freckles across her nose and smelled like cinnamon Tic Tac mints.

God, Tammy'd loved those things. She'd eaten them like candy. The memory was excruciating and sharp, slicing into his awareness.

The reality of his twin—the one person who had known him like no other—being irrevocably gone still shook him to the core. He could howl, he hurt so badly. Instead he bit down on what he really wanted to say to Max O'Neil.

He'd do anything to get inside that cave and take his mind off the pain for a while—except work with people who would compromise their own safety. He wasn't going to have someone else dying on him. That was the last thing he could handle.

"Yeah?" He stared deliberately at her long white fingers still resting on his sun-darkened skin, then he looked up with a raised eyebrow. He hated that he was attracted to someone who pissed him off so badly. But at her touch he gave in, deliberately surveying all of her, studying her as if he were memorizing the clothes she wore—the designer sandals, linen khaki capris, the now-transparent white top that stretched precariously across a very ample bosom.

She pulled her hand back as if she'd been burned.

"There's no room for negotiation on this, Dr. O'Neil." He leaned in closer to deliver the nasty one-two punch. "I don't care what kind of research you're doing. I explained it all to *your* boss earlier today. It was my only stipulation for taking the job. Caving safety rules will be followed at all times or I walk. Period. And I don't give a damn what you're offering."

Max O'Neil's head snapped back as if he'd slapped her. Finally her cheeks reddened in a deep blush. She cursed him under her breath.

He walked back to the overhang and the equipment, considering her anatomically impossible suggestion. *Not today, Red.*

"Zach, what are you doing?" Ellen whispered, shock evident in her tone.

He was grateful for both women's responses as they wouldn't hear his own heart pounding. He'd never been a very good poker player. Still, he was betting it all here. Michael was the only one who didn't look surprised, but he had been calling Zach's bluff since tenth grade. Don stood by the truck catching flies with his slightly gaping jaw.

Zach picked up another carabiner and line. He felt Max's eyes on him, boring a hole between his shoulder blades. No way she was winning this one. She couldn't possibly be as desperate as him.

He wanted into that cave and he wanted in with a cooperative group. Not someone he had to worry about going off on a tangent and killing herself over women's makeup for God's sake. He wouldn't take the job if that was the only way in. His heart, hell, his mind couldn't stand it.

He pulled the three harnesses from the bag that Ellen had dropped at his feet moments before and went to work rigging the ropes for the eight-gauge electrical line. He didn't so much as glance over his shoulder, but he could feel the daggers in his back. If Max O'Neil were armed, he'd be dead by now.

"You, Michael and I are the only ones going into Devil's Hollow today, Ellen." He handed her the empty duffel. "We're getting the batteries and the electrical line inside for Dr. O'Neil and her team."

"Zach, you can't talk to her like that." Ellen tried to whisper without moving her lips, doing her best ventriloquist impression.

He pretended he didn't hear her as he readied the first duffel of batteries and lighting equipment to be lowered into the shaft. Ellen gave O'Neil an apologetic shrug. The doctor stood watching them prepare to rappel into the cave, an unreadable expression on her face. Her silence bothered him.

"Call Kirk if you don't believe me," he suggested to Max as he passed her on his way to anchor another rope.

He heard her fumbling around in her purse behind him. "Oh, I intend to," she said loud enough for him to hear. "He's got some explaining to do," she muttered.

He walked back to the cave entrance and connected the descender to the line, preparing to step back into the tunnel opening.

"Wait a minute," said Max. "Are you going in dressed like that?"

He looked down at his clothes. Mud-caked jeans. Dusty knee pads. Hiking boots. Rain-soaked polypropylene T-shirt. His typical outerwear for Texas caving.

"What? You gonna loan me your sandals?" He was officially over the line, but this woman pissed him off like no one had in he didn't know how long.

She rolled her eyes and shook her head. "You can't go down there like that."

"Sure I can. I just snap into this harness and—"

"No, I mean, you have to have a biohazard suit on to go inside the cave. Stipulations of Earth Pharm's lease."

"What?"

"Do you wear deodorant, Mr. Douglas?"

"What does that have to do with—"

"Do you use fabric softener on your laundry, aftershave or hair gel of any kind?"

He shook his head. "I don't understand."

"They're all outside contaminants. The cave's a closed environment now and must remain so in order for us to duplicate the research Garrett sent up. It's critical. Anything we introduce into the cavern can upset the delicate ecological balance down there."

He looked at her like she was speaking Greek. "You want us to wear biohazard suits into this cave? Rappel down this shaft in that kind of gear?" *In your dreams, Red.* "That's insane."

The rain picked up as they stood glaring at each other.

Michael spoke for the first time. "Ma'am, it's almost a hundred-foot drop to the first chamber and another fifty-foot crawl through a tunnel to the main room before the half-mile hike to the pond you're interested in."

"There's more than one?"

Michael nodded. "It takes at least two hours from the time you step off the upper ledge here before you get to the water where Ellen got her samples. Don't you think the biohazard suits could wait until we get a little farther inside?"

"I'd kill myself before I got to the bottom," murmured Zach under his breath.

Max skewered him with those blue eyes again as a cool,

unfriendly smile slowly spread across her face. She'd obviously heard him. The temperature around them seemed to drop ten degrees. Suddenly Zach wasn't feeling so confident about his bluff.

"I can only hope." She shrugged and gave a small snorting laugh when she caught his shocked expression, throwing his own words back at him. "Ah, suck it up, Zach. You'll be fine."

# Chapter Three

The man's face would have been comical if Max hadn't been so angry. For five seconds he looked stricken and she felt a moment's remorse for being so awful. Then his green eyes went hard as emeralds and just as cold while he stared her down.

Distinctly uncomfortable, she took a deep breath. When he opened his mouth to speak, she heard the fury in his low, smooth voice. The sensual undertones had to be purely unintentional, but they threw her off balance.

"Dr. O'Neil, if you think for one moment that I'm going to sacrifice safety because you're pissed off about not being able to get into the caverns today, you can forget it. I'll quit first."

"Go ahead, I'm sure these people can handle it."

He cocked an eyebrow and shook his head. "Whatever you say, ma'am. You know everything about caving. I quit."

He untied the knots he was working on and stuffed the rope and harness into a bag before Max could speak. "Michael, Ellen, good luck here." He picked up more climbing gear and started packing it away.

Max, Michael and Ellen watched in stunned silence. When Michael walked forward to help him, Zach turned his back on Max to discuss the equipment dismantlement.

Before Max's eyes, climbing gear started to disappear into cavernous duffel bags. Ellen joined the men. Max could hear the woman's low, urgent whisper.

"Zach, are you sure?"

"I told Kirk I wouldn't do this if I had to deal with folks willing to sacrifice safety. I'm out of here. I'll call and tell him myself. The man assured me there wouldn't be a problem. Apparently he doesn't know his people as well as he thought."

Max was horrified. What had she done?

She'd been difficult, to be sure. But she'd had no idea the man would quit and take half the equipment with him. She stalked back to the Jeep and hauled herself inside. After a moment the teenage-chauffer followed her into the driver's side. She dug around in her purse for her BlackBerry and dialed Kirk's direct number while her head throbbed mercilessly.

*What the hell was going on?* Who was Zach Douglas and why in the world hadn't Kirk told her about him?

The Pied Piper answered on the second ring and she lit into him with all her pent-up fury. "Ralph, it's Max. What the hell's the deal here with Zach Douglas? He won't let me into the damn cave." *And now the man quit.* She wasn't ready to drop that bombshell.

"Relax, m'dear, he's your safety net. Just hired him today."

Damn. She could picture Kirk leaning back in his office chair sipping his tea now.

"He's a caver and can take care of the details you don't want to bother with. Now you can focus on getting the bacteria out of that cave for us."

"Well, I just met the man. And I'm not impressed."

"He comes highly recommended by the folks who found the bacteria and the National Park Service. He's supposedly one of the best cavers around. Besides, I think he can keep you and your team safe what with all the flooding in the surrounding caverns now. We don't know what's inside Devil's Hollow."

Wonderful, now she found this out. "Well, I think he's a control freak."

"What was he trying to control?"

She didn't answer.

"You?" Kirk's voice rumbled in her ear.

There was an uncomfortable silence. Finally she spoke up. "Who goes in or out of the caverns."

"I believe it takes a 'control freak' to know one. Look, why don't you let Zach Douglas do his job? I hired the man to keep you safe and, believe it or not, to lighten your workload. Trust him...." Kirk lowered his voice. "Just let him in, darlin'. And I don't mean tell him what we're really doing there, but he's not Robert, either. He can't hurt you like that."

She gave a noncommittal sound of acquiescence.

"Did you give him flak about wearing biohazard suits in the cave?"

"How did you—"

"I know you, Maxine. You're right and in a perfect world, you'd wear the suits. But practically speaking, you can't."

She started to argue, but he kept talking right over her.

"I know you got burned two years ago on that viral study, but you can't be a tight-ass about this where safety is concerned. Gloves only until you start culturing. That's a direct order from me as your boss, and I take full responsibility for the research consequences. I gave Douglas my word about safety. The man's rather a stickler about it, I'm afraid."

She sighed. When Kirk put on his "I'm the boss" hat all debate was over. "Yeah, you got that part right."

"So you really didn't get off to a good start with him?"

She took a deep breath and dove in headfirst. "He quit on the spot after meeting me. They're dismantling his equipment as we speak." She stared out the rain-streaked window at Zach loading his duffel bags into a truck.

"Good Lord, woman! What did you do? No, don't tell me. Let me guess, you were your own charming self."

She smirked into the phone. "'Fraid so."

"Well, hell, let me call the man and see what I can do about it. His one requirement for taking the job was that we adhere to all his safety standards. I assured him that wouldn't be a problem. You're going to have to apologize. Grovel more than likely."

"Kirk!"

"Don't even try to argue. I'll be sorry to miss the groveling. You do it so well, too…and so rarely."

She sighed, resigned to her fate. "I really put my foot in it, didn't I?"

"Honey, you jumped in up to your nose, I'm afraid. Apologize to the man. Be contrite." Kirk cleared his throat. "Afterward you can go have a large drink at the Lodge. Take it easy tonight. Hard work starts tomorrow. Not counting the sucking up you're about to do."

"Damn," she muttered under her breath. She really hated it when he was right.

"What's that, darlin'? I can't hear you."

"All right. I admit it. I screwed up big-time. You'll call him now?"

"As soon as I hang up with you. Give me five minutes before you go charm him."

"Yeah, and if you believe that, I have this bridge—" She punched the end-call button with more force than necessary and turned to Don, who'd been eavesdropping with unabashed curiosity to her side of the conversation.

"We're going to wait here for a couple of minutes." She shoved the BlackBerry into her purse and watched.

Zach was talking to Michael when his phone rang. Max watched his face as Kirk tried to schmooze him. God, she hated being in this position. No telling what Kirk was saying about her. Nothing less than what she deserved. She hated that even more.

She waited until Zach snapped his phone shut to make her move. He looked up as her car door opened. Green eyes zeroed in on her. She took a deep breath and hopped down out of the Jeep. Mud made an unpleasant squishing sound as she landed with a splat. An audible rendition of her life at the moment. For someone who truly despised apologizing, she'd spent an awful lot of time doing it lately. This was her own version of hell.

"Mr. Douglas, can we talk, please?"

His expression was unreadable. She held her head up and took a step forward, only to feel her sandal stick in the rain-soaked soil. The shoe came off and she fell to her knees, just catching herself before going face-first into a four-inch puddle.

She stayed crouched, dreading the moment she had to look up. Her hands were stinging and she was soaked from her toes to her shoulders. Beyond that, nothing was hurt but her pride. How in heaven's name had it gotten to this point?

Someone knelt beside her in the mud, gently taking her elbows. "Are you all right?" asked Zach.

He reached out and lifted her chin. His eyes weren't cold anymore. They were filled with concern and a touch of something she couldn't identify. Fear, maybe? That seemed ridiculous.

She swallowed hard and smiled. "I'm fine, just mortified. On top of being a jerk, I'm a klutz." He seemed surprised by her words and new attitude. She let him help her stand. He started to reach out to wipe the mud off her knees, but stopped himself before he touched her.

"I was coming to apologize," she said. "Please don't quit. Earth Pharm needs you on this project and obviously—" she opened her scraped hand to indicate the puddle he'd just helped her up from "—I need you on this, as well. Will you reconsider?"

He studied her a moment, resting a muddy palm on his hip. "You're difficult to read. You know that, don't you?"

She stared back, unsure of how to answer, then decided to go with the truth. "This isn't new information."

The truth must have worked because he said, "Apology accepted—on one condition. You buck me again on safety and I'm gone. I don't care what you say or what Kirk promised. Understand?"

She nodded and returned the hard gaze. "Just now? What did Kirk promise you?"

He smiled. "I think I'll let him tell you."

"What?"

"Nothing untoward, I assure you."

"No hints?"

He shook his head and grinned—and it was like plugging in a high-voltage bulb after sitting in a dark room all night. His face was transformed. Dimples, white smile, chiseled jawline. A stunning transformation from the man she'd met twenty minutes earlier.

"Just something I've wanted for a while."

Max struggled not to gape at the change in his demeanor. "Will I find out soon?" she managed.

"Call him back. He'll tell you."

"Okay, I'll do that. *Later.* I guess I'll go on to the Lodge." She headed toward the vehicle, her feet making an unpleasant sucking sound as she went.

Zach helped her up into the Jeep. His hand shot a bolt of awareness into her shoulder and straight to the pit of her stomach before she eased into the bucket seat. "I hope these can be hosed down," she muttered, uneasy at the sensations he was arousing in her.

"Don't worry about the seats. They've seen worse. It's a good idea for you to go on, though. You need to get out of those wet clothes."

She turned to Don, who'd never gotten out the second time.

"Can you please take me to where I'm staying tonight?"

He glanced over at Zach, who gave a barely perceptible nod. "Yes, ma'am. Right now?"

"Right now." She fastened her seat belt and prepared for the bone-jarring ride to wherever they were going. She caught herself glancing at Zach's hands and flashed on what they might feel like on her bare skin before she looked up at his face.

"I'll see you later, Max."

She swallowed and nodded, unsure if that was a threat or a promise.

MAX WRAPPED HER wet hair in the thin towel before donning her plush bathrobe. She had no idea it would be chilly here in early June. Apparently this was most unusual for the area and tough on one who slept in the nude. She'd slathered on lotion and pampered herself after a hot shower in the massive claw-foot tub, but now she was cold again. At least the Relpax was finally working, her headache backing off to manageable proportions.

Outside, the rain continued to fall. The wind whistled and beat against the stone walls of the Lodge.

Pulling on a second pair of socks, she shuffled into the quaint bedroom she'd been assigned. Mrs. Mabry, the "Lodgekeeper," had given her the scoop. The Lodge was built in the thirties and run by the state as part of the National Park system. An older couple usually ran things, but right now they were in Florida for the birth of their first grandchild, so Mrs. Mabry had been hired to take care of things.

Somehow Kirk had worked it out for Max and her entire team—including Zach and Michael—to stay here rather than in town. Ellen had asked to stay at her apartment because it was just fifteen minutes away. The Lodge was only open to special visitors of the park, so Earth Pharm must have made a hefty donation to Whispering Pines. The Lodge could use it.

The place was remarkable if not fully funded. Claw-foot bathtub. Antique furniture. But threadbare towels. The quilt on the brass and iron bed was lovely, a wedding-ring pattern of mauves, greens and blues.

Max wouldn't have cared if the spread was as ugly as sin. She was so tired, she could cry. Now if she could just sleep. Tomorrow was going to be unbelievably busy. All she wanted right now was to climb between the sheets and have the world go away. Even if only for six hours.

She pulled back the covers. Sitting on the edge of the bed, she slid out of her robe and tossed it on the desk. She started to put her feet under the quilt. That's when she saw it. Almost the size of her palm, dark peach-colored with a wicked black streak running down its back. The biggest, scariest scorpion she'd ever laid eyes on.

She screamed loud enough to shatter glass and leaped off the mattress. The towel tumbled from her head, but the scorpion remained perched in the center of the bed, unmoving. She stared, mesmerized, unable to back away.

Four seconds later, all hell broke loose. The outer door slammed against the wall as Zach and Michael burst through together. She hardly spared them a glance as she clutched the tiny towel to her chest, barely suppressing another scream as the scorpion slithered across the sheets and onto the floor. Finally her feet came unglued from the carpet and she was able to move at warp speed, her naked back slamming into Zack's chest.

"Umpfh." His arms came instinctively around her, his hands settling on her waist in an attempt to keep them both upright.

She shuddered at the unexpected full-body contact. Her bare backside landing squarely against his denim-clad thighs finally pulled her attention from the scorpion scurrying across the floor in the opposite direction.

"Are you okay?" She was so close to him, his words stirred the air behind her ear.

There was no graceful way out of this. She took a huge step forward and struggled with a towel that was barely big enough to cover her chest from one side to the other, much less wrap all the way around her. She hated to turn her back on the scorpion, but she couldn't moon Zach and Michael, either.

She pivoted on her socked heel and backed to the bed, desperate for a sheet or blanket. But she couldn't seem to get either to come loose from where they'd been seemingly stapled under the mattress. There was no longer any question about which side she'd rather have her naked butt exposed to. She grappled with the quilt and jerked an edge over her lap, keeping the towel over her breasts.

"Where is it?" she gasped, climbing on top of the bed and continuing to struggle with the quilt and sheets. "Do you see it? It crawled off as you came in. That scorpion was huge."

Both men met her eyes, an admirable task under the circumstances, and shook their heads.

# Chapter Four

"What? You must have seen it." She could hear the panic in her own voice. This was so not good. The two men looked at her like she'd lost her mind. She had to get a grip.

Zach and Michael deliberately scanned the floor, searching for the scorpion that appeared to be long gone. She could hear more people in the hall.

"You didn't see it?" she asked, the reality of the situation dawning. She was naked with a towel no bigger than a postage stamp to cover her and hair that must look like Medusa's, ranting about a scorpion. She tugged at the quilt with renewed vigor. It finally came loose from its ultimate hospital corners and she wrapped herself in a lopsided sarong in record time. Mooning your coworkers was highly frowned on in any workplace.

Sal Evans and Rodger Martin, two members of her team, were standing on her threshold, trying to come inside. "What's going on? Everything okay in there?" asked Sal. Max saw Tim Ryan behind Rodger.

"Max, you okay?" he asked.

Michael moved over to block the view, then stepped outside the room and pulled the door shut behind him, blocking out the voices, as well.

"Didn't you see it?" she asked again. Her voice broke and

her face flamed beet red; she could feel the flush working its way over her entire body.

Zach deliberately met her gaze and shook his head.

She closed her eyes. Hot waves of mortification rolled over her in ever-increasing intensity. She wanted to melt into the mattress.

"No, I didn't see a scorpion, but honestly, I was sort of distracted." There was a smile in his voice, but it wasn't condescending.

She forced herself to meet his stare. Nothing but concern was in his eyes. There was no hope but to brazen this out because it was beyond ridiculous.

"God, I have never been so embarrassed in my life. I don't usually make a habit of flashing the people I work with."

Zach nodded. "Well, I gotta admit I'm sorry to hear that."

A traitorous giggle bubbled up inside her.

Three hours ago, she'd hated this man. She knew he was only trying to make her feel better, but she had no idea how to answer him because what he said now bordered on flirting. At this point complete honesty seemed the only way to go.

"I have no idea what to say to you."

His dimples appeared. Was he trying to make her more comfortable or did he really mean what he was saying? She knew men liked looking at her body. She'd been a model, after all. The thought that he actually liked seeing her naked was so disconcerting she changed the subject.

"I think it went toward the bathroom." She pointed, still unwilling to leave her perch on the bed.

He nodded and headed for the doorway, grabbing the towel she'd dropped. From outside Michael knocked and opened the door.

"You find anything?" he asked.

There was the sound of something crashing into the sink, Max's toiletries most likely. The thwack of a towel hitting the bathroom wall. A muffled curse followed more scuffling, then silence.

Relief washed over Max like cooling ocean waves. Zach could completely destroy her bathroom at this point and she wouldn't care. As long as he saw the scorpion, too. At least he wouldn't think she was delusional. Seeing creatures where none existed.

Michael looked at her and raised an eyebrow. "You need any help?" He called out to Zach, but made no move toward the doorway. "Don't worry," he said to Max, "He's quite good at this."

"Chasing scorpions?"

Michael nodded. "You wouldn't believe the stuff he's gone after in the field. I once saw him grab a snake and fling it out of our tent."

Max's stomach clenched. "Lovely," she mumbled.

More shuffling emanated from the bathroom, then another loud *thwack* of a towel hitting tile. Zach appeared moments later with the towel wadded up.

"Did you get him?" asked Max.

"Yeah. But I'm not sure if he's dead or just stunned. I'll go toss him outside."

"I'll take him," offered Michael.

Zach handed over the towel.

"Why don't you just kill it?" asked Max.

"Why would I? Scorpions aren't bad for us, unless they sting you, of course. In fact in some ways they're good for the ecosystem out here. They're food for owls, lizards, bats, even mice."

"Bats?"

"You're a city girl, aren't you?" His green eyes were considerably warmer than they'd been this afternoon.

Max glared.

"Don't worry. Your scorpion was just doing what scorpions do. Skulking around."

"*My* scorpion?" Max wasn't happy. She was bloodthirsty.

"You're not buying this, are you?" asked Zach.

She shook her head. "I never wanted a scorpion that was 'mine.' I hate crawling things with a passion. Bugs, rodents. Bleck." She shuddered.

"You'll be fine. The ones here aren't poisonous. Just be sure to shake out your shoes before you put them on and check the blankets before you get into bed."

"Shake out my shoes?" She heard her voice rise and stopped herself from saying another word. Getting hysterical was not a good idea. She was already at a serious disadvantage here.

Zach raised an eyebrow. "Do you—" He stopped and watched her for a moment, lost in thought. She grew uncomfortable under his perusal.

"What?" she asked.

"Have you ever been in a cave before? Ever been camping?" The question wasn't meant as a challenge like it would have been this afternoon. "I don't mean this as a negative thing. I just need to know." He was genuinely interested, she could tell.

"I don't understand why you're asking me this." She stalled, but had a feeling she did know.

"I'm concerned that you aren't prepared for what's in store for you in Devil's Hollow."

She searched his face. There was no condemnation there. Just concern. "I know it's dark and close…that's all I thought I had to be worried about." She shuddered slightly. "I have an issue with small spaces."

Zach nodded. "Okay, I'll keep that in mind. But you need to know that there's more than small, dark spaces down there."

"What do you mean?"

"Well, there are critters in a few spots."

"Critters?" She heard her voice rise again. "What do you mean by that exactly?"

"Well, not exactly like what you had here tonight, but things that are not entirely dissimilar."

She took a deep breath. Well, hell. No one had told her about this.

"And there's one more thing."

*What else is left?* "Yeah?"

"There's been some flooding in the lower part of the cavern."

"Kirk mentioned that in passing this afternoon."

"The area has had record-setting rainfall over the past few weeks. All that water is seeping into the ground and into the aquifer. Some of the caves south of here are completely underwater. Because we don't know how deep Devil's Hollow is, we don't know what's happening inside. Ellen's pond is safe for now, but I'm not sure for how long if this rain keeps up."

"So I guess I'll have my work cut out for me?"

"In more ways than one. You okay with that?" He continued to stare, studying her response. His intent gaze made her extremely aware she was wrapped in only a quilt.

"Do I have a choice?"

"Well, probably not one you'd consider."

She knew what he was talking about and felt a frisson of dismay. The discussion had been going so well, too. "You mean not going into Devil's Hollow?"

He nodded.

She set her jaw, but kept her voice steady. She would not lose her temper. They'd made up too much ground tonight after their disastrous meeting earlier today. "Don't worry about me. I'll be fine."

"All right. But this isn't an endurance contest. You can come out whenever you want. Remember that. You're the boss."

As long as he remembered the last part, they would get along just fine. Scorpions notwithstanding. Her smile was brittle as she fought to keep it in place. "I'll keep that in mind."

Outside, a chilling wind continued to howl and rain hammered furiously against the window. Zach was surveying her again with a scrutiny that made her distinctly uncomfortable. She resisted the urge to check and make sure the quilt was covering her completely.

"Good." He nodded as if it were settled, but Max knew this particular part of the discussion was far from over. "Well, I'll leave you alone, then."

"Right." *Alone with my happy thoughts.* "Okay. I'll see you in the morning." She struggled not to stammer as he continued to bore a hole in her with his eyes.

"Hey," she protested softly. "Didn't anyone ever tell you that it's not polite to stare? Stop it." She put a hand up to shield herself from his intense perusal.

He shook his head with a bemused smile. "Sorry. It's nothing. It's just that you're so much like—"

A knock on the door interrupted him. Max wondered what he'd been about to say and who she reminded him of. A girlfriend? An ex-wife? He could be married, for all she knew.

"It's me, Michael. You okay in there?" He opened the door without waiting for an invitation and the moment was gone.

Max wasn't sure if she was relieved, disappointed or a little of both, but she smiled at Michael anyway. "Much better, thanks. I appreciate your disposing of the 'creature.'"

"Ah, well, Zach left the easy part for me." Michael walked to the bathroom, took a peek inside and cringed. "I think he left the hard part for you."

"Oh, yeah? What's in there now?" she joked.

Zach had the grace to blush. "Well, there was a small incident with the towel and your toiletries bag."

She shuddered on the inside, imagining a glass-covered countertop and floor.

"How much of it broke?"

"Broke?" Zach looked insulted. "None of it broke. I just dumped a lot of things on the countertop and into the sink." He grinned the high-wattage smile that took her breath away. "It's sort of cluttered in there right now. But everything is intact," he said, edging toward the door.

Michael laughed. "*Cluttered* is a generous term, Zach."

"I can help clean it up, but I didn't know if you'd want me

to." Zach was still moving toward the exit, obviously hoping she would say no.

Have his hands in all of her makeup, birth control pills and tampons? She shook her head. "I'll take care of it. As long as there're no scorpions, I'll be fine. You've done more than enough. Really. Thank you."

He left so fast, she barely had time to say good-night. Michael lingered a bit longer—obviously wanting to go, but unwilling to just walk out like Zach did.

"Was it something I said?" she wondered out loud.

"No, he just… He's that way sometimes." Michael leaned against the chest of drawers, looking distinctly uncomfortable.

"Really? Can you explain why?"

Michael glanced down, seemingly fascinated with the tops of his hiking boots. "He's in a tough place right now. He's not normally like he was today."

"That's an interesting thing to say about your friend. What's made him so different?"

Michael searched his feet for the answer a moment before looking up. "He, um…he lost his sister earlier this spring."

Max began to understand. "How sad. Was she ill?"

"No."

"A car accident?" A shudder of unease crept down her spine even as she asked. Somehow she knew the answer was more dreadful than an auto accident that arbitrarily steals away someone you love. There'd been something about Zach's intensity this afternoon.

"No." There was pain in Michael's eyes. "You'll hear about it sooner or later from the folks in town. I just didn't want to be the one to tell you, but maybe you'll understand Zach a little better. Cut him a little slack." He sighed, sounding bone-tired. Both men had been at the cavern for several hours after she'd gotten checked into the Lodge.

"Tammy was murdered. She was in the wrong place at the wrong time. It's been incredibly difficult for Zach." The sadness in his eyes would have spilled over if he'd allowed it to. "And I've said too much already."

*Maybe, but I think I needed to hear it.* "I'm sorry. You were close to her, as well."

"She was Zach's twin. They were a package deal." His hand was on the doorknob to leave.

"Thank you for telling me."

"If I were you, I'd want to know what I was getting into."

"What do you mean, *getting into?*"

But he was already closing the door quietly behind him and she wasn't quick enough in her makeshift sarong to stop him for further explanations.

*I SMILE AS I WATCH the computer monitor glowing in the dark. A woman wrapped in a quilt and a fully clothed man fill a quarter of the screen—their voices clearly audible. The three other squares are gray, indicating no movement in those camera ranges. Earlier I watched Zach Douglas thrashing about in Max O'Neil's bathroom, trashing the countertop, chasing a scorpion around the tiled floor.*

*The bombshell Michael just dropped is certainly rounding out the evening nicely. Everything has been orchestrated to keep the good doctor operating at less-than-optimum capacity. The committee demanded it play out this way.*

*It's somewhat gratifying to hear about Tammy Douglas. Who knew that job would have such far-reaching consequences? Apparently the butterfly principle is true. If a butterfly flaps its wings in China, you can indeed end up with a hurricane in the Gulf of Mexico or, as the case may be, here in the Texas Hill Country.*

*I lean back in my chair, studying the computer screen like a scientist studying slides under a microscope. A glass of single-malt whiskey rests at my elbow. I poured it at the beginning of the evening, but the glass is almost empty now. I can't have any more tonight. Nothing to dull the senses or the reflexes. Nothing to spoil the recollection of the evening's events. Who knew Max O'Neil could scream quite so loudly?*

*Every guest in the Lodge heard her.*

*And it's an interesting bit with O'Neil and Zach. Obvious who Max reminds him of. She looks just like Zach's dead sister. Not in a creepy way, but something about the way she carries herself. It's quite striking, even to me, who met Tammy Douglas only once.*

*Michael just left. The hidden cameras were placed well. The microphones, too. I could hear everything.*

*The doctor bites her bottom lip when she's unsettled. That's an interesting affectation. She's going to have a long evening. Sleep won't come quickly after finding that scorpion in her bed.*

*I'm glad I've hired people to handle other things tonight. I need to watch O'Neil's room. The camera is hidden directly behind the bed so that if she's cruising the Internet on her computer, I can see everything in the fisheye lens. The desk chair was deliberately moved out so the only well-lit place to work is on the bed.*

*It's of paramount importance that nothing goes unobserved in her world. As distasteful as some aspects might be. Hence the bathroom camera, as well. The committee insists on complete data. They want to know exactly what O'Neil is doing at any given time. Every scrap of info the woman gleans from Devil's Hollow has to be captured.*

*The committee won't stand for another failure of any kind. The stakes are entirely too high. I'm authorized to do whatever is necessary.*

*I contemplate my options and drain the glass. The whiskey burns on its way down. What is being considered is barbaric by some standards.*

*People who know me would be surprised to realize I have a conscience. But not about this. This business with O'Neil is...business. And nothing ever stands in the way of that.*

*The money is beyond belief and all I have in this world is
a reputation for delivering the goods, whatever it takes. So
no matter what, I'll do what is necessary. It doesn't matter to
me who gets hurt.*

# Chapter Five

The day dawned impossibly bright and clear, making it hard to believe the violent storms of the night before. The overhang entrance to the cavern had protected the ground from the fury of the rain, but mud still caked Zach's boots as he prepared to rappel into the cave's opening. The team of scientists wouldn't be arriving for a couple of hours, so he and Michael had some time to make an exploratory run before the job they'd been hired to do began. His private deal with Kirk kicked in now.

He rechecked the line before attaching the figure-8 to his harness. The bright sun dappled his head and shoulders until he was halfway down the rope, then disappeared completely as he landed on the floor of the vertical entry chamber. He glanced up to see Michael silhouetted above him.

"Hey, can you believe this day?" his friend called down.

Grateful Michael was here, Zach unsnapped the carabiner.

He'd been waiting for almost three months to get back. If he were really honest with himself, he'd been waiting the whole time he was enduring the pain of burying Tammy and dealing with the aftermath of her death. Thinking about mapping the rooms and exploring never-before-seen chambers had been a way to escape some of the pain of the past interminable weeks.

It was what he'd thought about while dealing with the irritation that was Earth Pharm yesterday. Although dealing with Max last night hadn't been such a pain.

The image of her bare skin and blush flashed across his consciousness like a beacon. He felt the corresponding response of his body. No, it hadn't been a hardship to watch her stammer apologies and flush from head to toe. Maybe that made him a chauvinistic creep, but having her backed up to him in all her naked glory last night had been right up there with the most fun he'd had in a very long time. Sort of went to show how bleak his sex life had been lately. Sadly, he couldn't get involved with her. He had some standards and he wouldn't sleep with a woman he didn't trust.

She was lying about something, he was sure of it. He trusted her and the company she worked for about as far as he could throw them. This job was a means to an end—exploring Devil's Hollow. Her body and her butt were off-limits.

"Hey, Zach, what's doing down there? Everything okay?"

"Damn." Zach breathed the curse, tightened his grip on the rope and snapped back to the task at hand. Fantasizing about Maxine O'Neil's ass could get him or someone else killed in this situation. "I'm fine!"

He unhooked from the rope at the bottom of the vertical chamber and belayed Michael down. One at a time, they squirmed through the fifty-foot tunnel on their hands and knees into the large waterfall chamber beyond. This would be easier going for the scientists than the hole in the ceiling he'd broken through earlier this spring.

Their plan was fairly simple. To get an overview of the cave, he and Michael would take rough surveys while they didn't have the scientists with them. It might not be perfectly accurate, but they'd have an idea of what was here. While the scientists were working and doing their own research, he and Michael could take detailed measurements of the various rooms they were working and waiting in. After Earth Pharm's lease was up, Zach hoped to come back and survey at leisure.

Zach glanced toward the corner where he and Michael had staged the equipment yesterday. Several duffels containing battery-powered lights and other gear for a field lab had been stacked under a tarp.

Zach did a double take. The tarp was missing.

"What the hell?" he muttered under his breath. "Michael, we covered that equipment last night before we went up, right?"

Michael looked at the stack of bags, as well. "Yeah, I remember thinking it was a little silly, but we did it."

"That's what I was afraid of. Someone's been down here."

"You sure?"

"Well, those tarps didn't just levitate. There's no other way they could have moved unless someone jacked with them." And messed with the equipment. He looked around.

The sound in the chamber was muffled by the rushing waterfall at the far end. The surrounding walls were so thick, they might as well have been in a soundproof booth. There was no way to tell if they were alone down here or not.

"You think whoever did it is gone?" asked Michael.

"I'm almost positive." Zach shrugged. "No ropes in the entry tunnel except ours."

"Or they're working with someone." Michael looked around the room and shuddered. "Creepy," he muttered.

"Yeah. Is the gear okay?" Zach opened the first bag and got his answer. The battery pack for the portable lights was cracked, punctured with a tiny hole. A thin liquid trail of battery acid had leaked into the rest of the bag. Everything the acid had touched was slowly bubbling, or buckling. An unholy mess.

"Damn it." The entire contents of this bag were shot.

Michael stepped beside him. "What do you think happened?"

"I have no idea." Zach shrugged. "What about your bag?"

Michael shook his head.

He gingerly picked up a field microscope, and silver shards of glass made a musical tinkling sound as they slid out of the long metal cylinder and back into the open duffel.

Zach stared at the ruined equipment. "Do you know exactly what it is that Earth Pharm is working on?"

"Not really. Something to do with mineral research and Ellen's thesis at UT. She had to sign a nondisclosure agreement, so she's been pretty evasive. The folks from Earth Pharm said it has something to do with a new women's makeup and revolutionary technology. That's why it's so hush-hush."

"Hmm. All this for women's makeup? I don't think so."

"What do you mean?"

"Look at this mess. I can't believe someone would sabotage a cosmetic research team like this. Doesn't smell right. Why wouldn't Earth Pharm tell us what they're really doing here?" asked Zach.

"Trade secrets?" suggested Michael.

"Maybe." Zach studied the bags of ruined gear again. "Why wouldn't someone want Earth Pharm to do their cosmetic research here?"

"Don't want them to get the corner on the mineral makeup market?" Michael grinned.

"Could be," said Zach. "Or could just be some delinquent kids horsing around."

"You don't believe kids did this?"

Zach shook his head. *There are a lot of things about this I don't believe.* "Nope, just trying to think positive here."

"What do you mean?" Michael took a drink from his water bottle.

"If it's not kids, we're in way over our heads and completely screwed."

MAX PULLED A long-sleeve T-shirt over her head and tucked it into jeans before gulping down the strong coffee. After the scorpion fiasco of last night she hadn't slept a bit and had ended up on eBay till all hours bidding on a Royal Doulton mug. She was down $230 but the proud new owner of an exquisite mini Queen Elizabeth Toby jug from 1945. She'd have her Tudor collection complete again, damn Robert's hide.

She caught a glimpse of herself in the dresser mirror. Dark circles and bags that needed porters hung under her eyes. No one would accuse her of being on a spa vacation.

Refusing to be late her first day, she scraped her hair back and quickly washed her face. She'd met with Sal and the rest of the team yesterday after dinner. The others were just as excited about this project as her, but she was the youngest person from Earth Pharm by at least five years.

Rodger Martin, Salvatore Evans and Tim Ryan were all in their late thirties. Max was the only woman, plus she was in charge. Her conduct had to be exemplary. Lord. She shook her head again over the peep show of last night. Well, she was going to have to suck it up, make a joke if necessary and go on.

Not that she expected anyone to give her trouble. Everyone on the team—hell, everyone at Earth Pharm—had been touched by cancer in some way. Who in this day and age hadn't? They were all anxious to start, but she wasn't naive enough to forget that careers were going to be made here, as well.

She slid into a Day-Glo green Gortex jacket and slung a matching daypack over her shoulder. Slamming the door behind her, she heard the automatic click of the lock. She walked at a fast clip toward the stairs and saw Tim coming out of his room.

He gave her a tentative smile. "You ready to get started?"

"Absolutely. It's going to be exciting."

"I hope so." He sounded unsure, which was quite unlike him. "I'm not much for small spaces," he muttered.

Max smiled like a kindergarten teacher on the first day of school. *Uh-oh. Not you, too.* "Yeah, I understand." *More than you know.* "Ellen told me it's a fairly large area where we're working. Not claustrophobic at all." She didn't add that getting there was a bit of a tight squeeze.

"We'll be fine." Max wasn't sure if she was saying that for her benefit or Tim's.

"Right," he mumbled, definitely not convinced.

"Where's everyone else?" she asked. They'd arrived at the bottom of the stairs to find an empty lobby.

"The guides are at the cave already. Left early this morning. The rest of the team is outside with our driver, Don. I just came back in to brush my teeth."

"Oh." Max's stomach gave a mighty roar as she passed the buffet area. She stopped to snag a muffin and stuff some fruit in her pack. This would have to do for breakfast. She looked for the rest of the team through the bay window. Seeing no one, she assumed they were already waiting in the Jeep. "All right, then. Let's go."

She swallowed a bite of the muffin, started for the front door and tugged on the heavy wrought-iron pull. The door slowly swung open. "It's a beautiful da—"

Three men stood on the front porch dressed in jeans and flannel shirts. One was in the act of raising his hand to knock on the massive oak door. Max stepped back.

"Dr. O'Neil?" The voice was slow, Southern. Two of the men were older, while the other appeared to be in his midforties.

"Yes?" Max looked from one to the other in startled surprise.

The youngest apparently was the spokesperson for the group. "We're on the city council of Reddington and we'd like to welcome you and Earth Pharm to the area."

Alarm bells went off in Max's brain as she sought to keep a perfectly placid expression on her face. "Thank you. I must say this is totally unexpected. How did you know that we were in the area?"

One of the older gentlemen spoke up. His voice had more of a Texas twang. "Why, the community has been positively abuzz since we heard Earth Pharm had leased the land from Paul Tillman. We assumed you were coming to take a look at the new caverns. We understand there is some mineral research involved."

Max raised an eyebrow. Even if these men looked like an ad for Countrytime Lemonade, they were by no means slow.

"We want to know when you intend to open the cave." This was from the younger councilman.

"Pardon me?"

"As you may have noticed, Reddington is somewhat depressed economically. The publicity could give us a much-needed shot in the arm."

How in the world had she stepped into such a pile?

PR wasn't her job. She sucked at it. But she was a helluva scientist. She'd never wished for Kirk and his silver tongue quite so fervently. If possible, she had to extract herself without stepping on any local toes.

"Gentlemen, I can't say at this time when the cave will be open. We haven't even begun our survey of the caverns yet. As you can see—" she pointed to the carload of people. "—we're on our way there right now. So if you'll just excuse me…"

One of the men stepped in front of her. He wasn't menacing, but he was blocking her progress all the same. "Dr. O'Neil, do you intend to open the cavern when your preliminary survey is done?"

"I'm sorry, I can't really say." Which everyone, especially these very sharp, non-country bumpkins knew meant no.

She deliberately stepped around the three men, willing Tim to follow her, dreading the next logical question that would come if she gave these men time to ask it. The bright morning suddenly seemed tarnished and dismal. She smelled rain on the breeze.

Tim didn't catch on as quickly as Max had hoped and slowed down getting past the town inquisitors.

"What is it exactly that Earth Pharm is doing in Devil's Hollow? We'd heard it was mineral research. Does that mean gemstones? Diamonds?" The older gentleman's questions stopped Max before she opened the car door.

*Where had that come from?* This was not the turn they expected or needed in their cover story. She avoided a large puddle and turned to smile apologetically. "No, I'm sorry. You're mistaken. We're researching a new mineral for a women's makeup line."

The man looked at her skeptically. "Hmm. That's not what I heard."

She shrugged.

"Can you tell us more about it?"

"I'm sorry. I'm not at liberty to discuss it at this time. I hope you understand."

"No, ma'am, I'm afraid I don't. You won't tell us what you're doing up there and you won't tell us if we'll be able to open the cave for the tourism this area desperately needs."

*No, it's not at all likely.* If Max found what she was hoping to, very few people outside of Earth Pharm employees would ever see the inside of Devil's Hollow. But she couldn't tell him that.

This was the price for secrecy. And she didn't care for it. Instead, she continued to smile like the chairman of the board who knows he's about to lay off half the company but isn't telling yet. "I'm sorry. My hands are tied."

"Well, I assure you, ours are not. The lease deal with Paul Tillman is up in six weeks, is it not?"

Well, hell. She was paralyzed a moment before turning up the wattage on her smile. "Yes, I believe so."

"So in six weeks the contract can be renegotiated with anyone?"

She gave another noncommittal shrug as her throat tightened. "I suppose you would have to talk to Mr. Tillman about that."

"You can count on it. Good day to you, Dr. O'Neil." With that the men turned and left her staring after them with a plastic beauty-queen smile plastered on her face and acid reflux simmering in her stomach. Sal and the others climbed out of the Jeep as the councilmen stalked to their vehicle.

Good Lord, Kirk would have apoplexy, heart failure. Probably both. It was much more serious than her blowing things with Zach yesterday and she'd done nothing to upset these men. But diamonds? This was not the cover story Earth Pharm wanted circulating. And she couldn't tell them the true nature of the research.

That, of course, was the root of the problem. She couldn't tell anyone what was really going on. The price for secrecy had just increased exponentially.

"WELL, THAT WAS fun," said Max. The other team members stood around her watching the councilmen drive away.

"I'm sorry," said Tim. "I should've seen that coming."

Max shook her head. "No, I've been expecting it. But I am surprised they knew we were here already. I'd hoped to avoid it for a while. It's why we're staying out here instead of in town."

They watched the rapidly disappearing vehicle, then climbed back into their own Jeep.

Feeling all eyes on her, Max turned in her seat.

"So what are you going to do?" asked Rodger.

This was it. The moment of truth. They wanted to see what kind of decision maker she was.

She worried her bottom lip with her teeth before she spoke.

"We're gonna hang tight. We knew we'd get a little community interest at some point, not that I was expecting the diamond rumor. I'll let Kirk know. For now, we've got a job that has nothing to do with lease issues, tourism or misconceptions. What we need to focus on is the research."

The three men all stared at her for a moment.

Finally, Sal spoke up. "Yes, you're absolutely right." And apparently, that was that. They began talking about the project in guarded terms. What they'd do first. How they should gather the samples. What the cave's atmosphere would be like. No one in the group had ever been spelunking before.

Max turned around and surveyed the passing scenery. It felt so different from other times. She'd always had to fight for her point of view. If this was any indication, the group was going to be a real pleasure to work with. Maybe she needed to strip down and scream bloody murder the night before the start of every big project.

Twenty minutes later they were at the cavern's entrance. Two trucks were parked out front just like yesterday.

As they drove in, Don honked the horn. "Depending on where Zach and Michael are in the cave, they'll hear us and know we've arrived. They're expecting us about this time." He grinned at her.

As they were getting out of the Jeep, Michael was climbing out of the yawning hole in the ground with a duffel bag. Several duffels with Earth Pharm logos were stacked beside the entrance. He was bringing the bags *up* from the cave?

A flat rock overhang protected the point of entry from most of the elements, almost like a covered patio. Everyone piled out of the Grand Cherokee and wandered slowly to the small mountain of gear. Zach was climbing out of the ground as everyone stepped into the shade.

Michael gave him a hand up just as Tim Ryan was bending over one of the bags.

"Don't touch that," growled Zach. "It's evidence."

"Evidence of what?" asked Sal.

Max stared at the duffels. Two had bluish-green stains on them. Her optimistic mood vaporized.

"Someone was down there yesterday, after we left. They tampered with your lab equipment," explained Zach.

"What do you mean tampered with it?" Max ignored Zach's earlier protests and bent to open the bag nearest her.

Their time was so limited. Salvaging damaged gear was much more important than prosecuting vandals. They didn't have the luxury of days to process evidence.

She unzipped the duffel. Glass covered the carefully packed apparatus. Battery acid leaked over sterile specimen jars. Feeling slightly ill at the waste, she exploded. "Tampered with it? They destroyed it!"

"How did they get in?" demanded Rodger.

"Same way we did. There's no way to lock anyone out at this point. Unless—"

"Unless you hire a night watchman," finished Max, trying to calm herself.

"Which is what I suggest you do once you replace the equipment. I can't guarantee this won't happen again."

"Good Lord." Sal Evans leaned against the rock face. "First the councilmen, now this."

"What councilmen?" asked Zach.

"Three councilmen came to the Lodge today asking Max when the cavern would be open to tourists. When she told them she didn't know, they indicated they'd be talking to the owner about leasing the land themselves. Plus they think we're mining gemstones, diamonds."

"That's insane. Diamonds aren't even a remote possibility in this kind of formation," said Zach.

"Diamonds only form in kimberlite pipes," explained Michael. "Devil's Hollow doesn't have those."

"But even operating under that huge misconception, I still don't see how they could have had anything to do with this. They wanted you to let them in. They didn't know the answer was going to be no until this morning. This was done last night or sometime very early this morning." Zach undid the buckles on his climbing harness.

"What are you researching that would have people sabotaging you?" He stepped out of the harness and looked up at her.

Max stopped her gentle rifling through the bag as the entire team stared at him. It was like being at a party that's going really well, then suddenly someone commits a gross social faux pas and the room goes dead quiet.

Max broke the silence. "It's mineral research for women's make—"

Zach held up his hands to cut her off. "Never mind. We just won't ask and you won't have to lie."

Her face turned bright red, but she couldn't argue.

Michael filled the awkward silence. "So, what do you do now?"

Max brushed her hands off on her jeans. "I'll call Kirk for new equipment. He can have some here by tomorrow. As for the rest of the day, I'm not sure."

She watched Rodger Martin pulling damaged gear gently out of the bag, treating it like a newborn baby. It was quite a dichotomy because the man was built like a linebacker. He'd not said a word on hearing about the vandalism. And he'd completely ignored Zach's orders to leave the damaged duffels for evidence. He'd immediately pulled a tarp from one of the bags and set to work inventorying the destruction.

"You think anything there can be salvaged?" she asked.

"I need to get the battery acid off as much of this stuff as possible. Some of the stainless-steel lab tables can definitely be saved."

"Tell us what to do, Rodger. You're the equipment wrangler," said Max.

"We need gloves to work, so no one's hands will get damaged by the battery acid. If we double or triple glove, it should work."

"Well, I'm pretty sure the gloves are safe," said Zach, pulling a plastic package of safety gloves from the third bag. "No batteries in this bag."

"See, I told you we'd need tho—" Max stopped. *Damn.* She wanted to bite her tongue. Gloves. The cause of all that contention yesterday.

"I'd never have believed it." Zach shook his head and tossed her the box. There was humor in his voice. She fumbled the package and looked up. That *GQ* smile of his almost caused her to drop the carton.

He continued, unaware of the effect. "There's water and a galvanized bucket in the back of Michael's truck. Mr. Tillman would be okay with us using the water hose by the cow trough to refill that big cooler if we use all of our own water and need more."

Michael spoke up. "I'll call Ellen to bring more paper towels when she comes after her class."

Max swallowed the lump in her throat that had nothing to do with thirst. "Sounds like a plan."

Soon everyone had donned gloves in triplicate and was gently removing damaged gear from the duffel bags. It took an hour, but they finally made some progress.

Max stood and stretched her back. She walked away from the group and punched Kirk's number into her cell. This morning had put her way out of her depth.

Kirk picked up on the third ring. "Hello, Maxine. What's up?"

She took a deep breath. "Apparently a little sabotage."

"Explain yourself, darlin'."

She gave him the details of the morning—from the councilmen's visit to a description of the cleanup process taking place before her eyes.

"We have one microscope and seven unbroken sterile specimen jars. Rodger has the microscope on the tailgate of Zach's truck and is checking it out as we speak. If that's working we could actually get into the cave today for a while. But we don't have battery backups for our lights."

"Will Zach let you go down there with that?"

"I don't know."

"Well, if he will, go ahead. You need to get a feel for it if nothing else. I'll have new equipment shipped out today. It'll be there by 8:00 a.m."

"Zach said a night watchman is the only way to guard from this happening again."

"I agree. We'll see about hiring one right away. Keeping our research private has become even more important."

"I understand."

"You can't tell anyone."

"Yes, Kirk, I get it."

"Not even the men who are helping with the caving."

Max felt the irritation wash over her. "Right. I understand." She ground her teeth. He was perfectly within his boundaries to be checking her on this, but she was still irritated.

"Things sound like they're going a bit sideways there. Do you feel you're not up to the task?"

Max didn't breathe. One of her favorite expressions and now he was turning it around on her.

"No, no, I can do it. I just don't necessarily like it."

"Yes, well, darlin', I didn't think you would."

*Right.*

"Call me if you need anything else."

He hung up abruptly and she was left staring at the men working on the equipment. She'd needed Kirk's advice. Truth be told, Max might even need him here. And that burned a little. Hell, it burned a lot. Even though everyone was working so well together, this latest event put a new twist on things and made her uneasy.

Was the vandalism really just the act of disgruntled citizens or was there something else going on? There was no way to know at this point.

She plastered on a smile and walked back to join the others.

"So, Zach, are we going down today?"

He raised his head and looked her over in a way that reminded her he'd seen her wearing nothing but a threadbare towel last night.

*Oh God, someone just shoot me now.* She swore she wasn't going to blush at the silly junior-high double entendre she'd just uttered. Still, she could feel a flush start at the roots of her hair and travel down her neck and chest.

"Are you sure you're up for that?" asked Zach. He was staring as he had last night in a way that made her distinctly uncomfortable.

She was going to have to brazen this out and act like she hadn't just said the most asinine thing in the world. And she'd do that, once she could breathe again. She took a gulp of air. "Absolutely."

Zach kept piercing her with those green eyes. It was obvious he was trying to figure her out.

*Yeah, good luck with that.*

"All right, if nothing else, we can get you and your team used to the feel of the equipment. It can be an adjustment," he said.

Was everyone looking at them or was it just her overactive imagination and libido? "I'm sure I'll be able to handle anything that comes up down there."

His pupils dilated ever so slightly as she desperately wished those words back.

"You're the boss." He smiled and her breath caught.

Oh, good Lord. When had she lost control of her brain and her mouth so completely? She'd never made suggestive comments to men she worked with and now she'd done it twice in less than forty-five seconds. He had to think she was coming on to him.

*Great.* Between this man, her claustrophobia and a sudden case of foot-in-mouth disease, she'd be begging for someone to put her out of her misery before the day was over.

# Chapter Six

Zach had his hands on Max as he tightened her harness and helped her practice in preparation for sliding down to the floor of the entry chamber. They'd been all over each other and in all kinds in interesting positions for the past twenty minutes as he showed her how to rappel and get into her gear. Still, it was all within a professional capacity. Plus they'd had an audience—her team and his.

As Zach reached around Max to triple-check her harness, he had to remind himself again what he was doing here. Michael should be showing her how the descender worked, but he couldn't stand the thought of seeing Michael's hands on her.

What the hell was wrong with him? Yesterday he'd wanted the woman gone. As far away from him and *his* cave as possible. She was lying through her teeth to him about what Earth Pharm was doing here. But it didn't seem to matter anymore.

When had this happened? Last night when she'd backed into him in all her bare-assed glory? Why was she getting to him so? The suggestive comments she'd made earlier hadn't helped. Although he was pretty sure they were unintentional, if the look on her face after she'd made them was any indication.

Shaking his head to clear away the erotic images those words had called to mind, he tightened his own harness and stepped off the ledge. Slowly he left the surface to rappel into the quiet of the vertical entry chamber. Green lichen covered the rocky walls. The cool air and quiet calm of a cave never failed to surprise him. He felt the frenzy and frustration of the past two hours fall away as he stood on the limestone floor. The mineral scent of the walls permeated the air. He'd take bets his blood pressure dropped when he caved. Better than beta-blockers, but not sex, his libido chimed in.

While Rodger, Ellen and Don stayed topside, Max and her crew landed beside him in various states of athletic inability. Sal and Tim were going to require some watching, but Max seemed fairly comfortable with the equipment and the techniques. All three scientists were fascinated with the entry chamber. The group patiently took turns crawling through the long tunnel to get to the larger room beyond.

The waterfall and pool awed everyone just as they had Zach the first time he'd seen them.

The way to Ellen's pond was a grueling two-hour hike over uneven ground with sloping low ceilings that involved a trek over a stone bridge and another slithering crawl through a tunnel of mud. The only sound was the constant dripping of water and the distinct sound of rushing water that grew steadily louder the deeper they walked into the caverns.

They passed the first two of three crevasses and had a scary moment on the third when Sal Evans lost his footing and slipped on the ledge approaching the target pool. Zach caught him just before he slid into a hole that could have meant a very bad day.

The scientists were a game bunch. But Zach was still wondering if this was a good idea when they rounded the corner to Ellen's bacteria pond.

One large, still, clear pond.

Max was the first to speak. "I imagined this as some mold-encrusted body of water. I never thought of it as being so unbelievably clear. You can't really see the water."

Zach nodded. "There aren't any particles that allow you to see depth."

"Why not?"

"Bacteria oxidize them. Eat them. That's what keeps the water so incredibly unclouded."

"So how deep is it?" Max asked

"Not sure," admitted Zach. "They haven't wanted to measure for fear of contaminating the water in this particular pool."

Max shot him a questioning glance.

"We aren't Neanderthals, Dr. O'Neil, even though you might think so. Several of the other ponds here are between twelve and nineteen feet deep. This one appears to be about the same depth."

Tim leaned forward at the edge, looking down. His boot was on the edge of a rock, dangerously close to the pool. "This is so freaking clear. Amazing."

Sal took one look at Tim's foot and growled. "What the hell are you doing, man? Trying to sabotage us? Watch where you put those size-thirteen boats of yours."

Tim smiled over his shoulder and leaned farther down to look at the water. His backpack slid to the side and rested on the rocks beside him. Zach was fascinated by the exchange. Max sidled over to Sal, trying to soothe the disgruntled scientist. "It's all right. He's not going to fall in."

"I hope not. You of all people know what would happen if he did."

Max nodded. "We'd be having a helluva short stint here. You wouldn't have to worry about those biohazard suits, Zach, even if it was just his big toe going for a swim. We'd be pretty much screwed in terms of duplicating our research."

"What do you mean? Did something happen before?" asked Zach.

Sal exchanged a pained look with Max. She nodded and Sal started talking in his gravelly voice. "Two years ago at another company, Max and I were about to start the clinical trials for a new drug. The project had been running for fifteen years. I was a kid when they started the research."

He shook his shaggy head. "Anyway, three weeks before the viral drug trial was to start, Max realized there had been contamination of test samples by one of the founding scientists in the first stages of the project ten years earlier. He hadn't worn gloves during some of the initial testing. All the work was totally corrupt. God, it was awful."

Michael whistled long and low. "Fifteen years. Wow. That had to cost some money."

"Eighty-five million, eight hundred thousand, nine hundred forty-two dollars and fifty-three cents...Oh, and both our jobs. All for want of some latex gloves."

"Your jobs?" asked Zach. Jesus. No wonder Max had been so adamant about the biohazard suits. That would mark you no matter what you were researching.

"Corporate America does not care for whistle blowers. They'd generally rather take their chances in court. Most litigants give up or run out of money long before the courts reach a finding against a pharmaceutical company," said Max.

"It's David and Goliath," said Tim.

"No kidding," muttered Zach.

"But I'm not bitter." Max smiled. "That experience brought me to Kirk's company. I never would have gone to work for him if I hadn't been fired."

Michael barked a laugh.

"Well, that didn't come out exactly how I meant it. I mean, we were too good of friends and I didn't think I could work for him. We were too close. But it's been really good. A completely different ball game from PharmaVax."

"You used to work for PharmaVax, the anti-Christ of pharmaceutical companies?" asked Michael.

Zach stared at her, hardly believing.

"Yes. I didn't know what they were when I first took the job. I needed the money and it was great work."

Zach was in shock. She'd worked for the same company responsible for Tammy's murder. The coincidence was so disturbing, he had to turn away to compose himself. He watched Tim, who was still leaning over the pond. He noticed that the light attached to his headgear was slowly sliding forward off the helmet. If the battery-powered light fell into the water, this gig was over before it started.

"Your headlamp," he shouted. Tim looked up in confusion as Zach tackled him from the side. The light flew backward and cracked against the boulder behind them.

"What the hell?" Tim pushed Zach off and was about to throw a punch, but Michael was there helping them up before they'd even gotten untangled.

"Your headlamp was about to go for a swim in the pool," explained Michael, playing peacemaker.

"Couldn't you have just said something instead of pretending to be a linebacker?"

Zach knew an explanation would be pointless.

"Well, no broken bones, at least." Only bruised egos.

Tim gave him a hard stare and turned back to his pack to pull out the little bit of equipment they'd salvaged for gathering samples from the pond. Zach walked away to the other side of the pool.

Max stopped on her way past him and spoke in a low voice. "You did the right thing. Tim'll realize it, too. Once he gets over being embarrassed for almost destroying the pool."

Zach appreciated that, but didn't know what to say to her, either. So he merely shrugged again.

The sound of running water was loudest at this end, but the pond was completely still.

"What's that sound?" asked Sal.

"The Edwards Aquifer. It's recharging at a higher rate than usual because of all the rain."

"Recharging?" asked Sal.

Michael explained in full tour-guide mode. "Think of the aquifer as a bucket of water that the cave is sitting on top of. As it rains, the ground water seeps down into the bucket. If the bucket is full, the aquifer will overflow into the passages of the cave."

"So is this cave flooding?" asked Sal.

Zach folded his arms and watched Michael tap dance around the answer.

"The whole region gets its water from these underground streams in one way or another. The Edwards Aquifer runs under this cavern."

"You didn't answer the question," said Sal. "How long before this cave floods?"

Zach stepped in to answer. "The caves south of here are completely flooded from all the rain this year. That's very unusual. Not having been in Devil's Hollow before, we don't know what the situation is like farther in."

Sal cut to the chase. "So how much time do we have to finish the research?"

Zach exchanged a look with Max before answering. "I don't know that it's critical in terms of time. This cave could be several miles deep for all we know. Bottom line, we aren't sure of our timeline here. Without a survey of Devil's Hollow, we have no way of knowing the depth and how close we are to flooding until the water appears—unless we go looking for it ourselves. That's why Michael and I were down here earlier today."

"What did you find?" asked Sal.

"Unfortunately we didn't get past the vandalism."

"So why don't you go check things out now?" suggested Max. "I realize you can't go far, but we should be okay here for a little while. That water sounds pretty close."

Zach looked at Michael. "You up for it?"

Michael grinned. "Always."

Zach picked up his pack. "All right. Let's go in for thirty minutes and then turn back if we aren't to that first source. It'll be worth it to take a look." He glanced back at the group of scientists enthralled by the pool. They were preparing to glove up and go to work gathering samples from the pond.

"What kind of trouble can they get into here?" asked Michael.

"Don't say that," warned Zach. "I think we just saw what could happen." He walked over to give face-to-face instructions. "We'll be back in thirty minutes. No one leaves this chamber."

Tim and Sal didn't stop working. Max barely glanced up before tending to her syringes and specimen jars. "Where would we go?"

"I have no idea, but you'd find some kind of trouble to get into. I've no doubt."

She raised her face then, and he could read the skepticism there.

"Dr. O'Neil, check your watch. Thirty minutes. Mark it. We're working on an issue here with powering the lights. If for some reason we're not back, stop working and turn off your headlamps. You'll have to conserve the battery packs. That way we'll have enough power to get out of here. Do you understand?"

That got her attention. She met his gaze and he saw the frisson of unease in her blue eyes. Apparently, the thought of being stuck in a dark cave with no light source was her undoing. Welcome to every caver's nightmare.

Finally, she checked the time on her clunky watch. "Yes, I've got it."

He nodded. "Good. See you in a few."

TWENTY-FIVE MINUTES later they were back. The news wasn't good. Zach had never seen water rising quite that fast before in a cave. He was going to keep that news to himself until absolutely necessary. But these folks were going to have to get their research done fast.

"What did you find?" asked Max.

"There's a chamber directly below us with a large stream and fast-moving water. I can't tell how quickly it's rising, but the water is definitely coming up. We put out a homemade marker to check later. We don't have enough time left on the batteries for a good safety margin. It's better to go back now than to get stuck here with no light," he said.

The scientists packed up and everyone headed out. Sal carried the samples with Michael in the lead. Max, Tim, then Zach brought up the rear. Tired, muddy and achy from walking stooped over for several hundred yards at a time, they traversed the uneven ground.

When it happened, they were twenty minutes from the vertical entry chamber. Tim was crossing a narrow, sloping stone bridge; two hundred feet below, water rushed through a deep stone canyon. Maybe he'd gotten careless because they were close to home. Zach was never sure.

Tim slipped on the damp, mossy surface. It was so fast the others didn't see him go over. Initially, he didn't even shout. He just went down hard. Zach heard a sickening crack as the man slid sideways to the edge of the natural bridge. Then Tim was screaming and desperately grabbing for the rocky out-cropping while he slithered down the side.

Tim held on by his fingertips as Zach lunged for him, struggling for his wrists. Zach caught one hand. Tim clutched desperately with his other, bellowing and thrashing. Zach felt as if his arm was being ripped out of its socket, but he held on. There was no choice. It was a drop into sheer nothingness when he looked over the ledge.

## Chapter Seven

"Don't move, Tim." Zach's palms were slick from his skid over the damp moss. Tim was panicking and flailing about. "Stop it, man, or you'll slide right out of my hands." Zach slid forward with his arms and chest hanging over the edge. "Be still."

Then, thank God, Michael was there, lying on his belly beside Zach and reaching down to grab Tim's other arm. Together they pulled Tim up and off the stone bridge. Sal was there, too, holding on to both of their legs so no one else slid off the ledge. Tim rolled into a fetal position once he was on the ground and Sal started checking his leg. Zach recalled the crack he'd heard as Tim went down.

He looked up and met Max's eyes. Something had changed there. She'd stood back out of the way during the episode. He walked over to check on her. Her face was as white as the flowstone around them.

"It happened so fast, I didn't see it. The others didn't see it. We wouldn't have known if you hadn't shouted." She was babbling.

"Oh, you'd have known."

Zach studied Max's face for a moment. Tense didn't begin to describe her. She was standing so rigidly straight he would bet she'd tip over if he pushed her. That or simply break in two. This had freaked her out beyond what he would have expected. Something in her eyes finally clued him in, and he realized she was on the verge of panic.

Unobtrusively, she was taking quiet sips of air, trying not to show how terrified she was. It wasn't working.

She looked at Tim again. Michael had him laid out near the ledge and was talking to him as he looked him over. Sal was cleaning Tim's bloody hands with water. Max made no move to walk over to them. That's when Zach got it. She was scared to death.

Heights, claustrophobia. He wasn't sure which, but Dr. O'Neil was ready to come out of her skin. And he'd better get to the bottom of it before they crossed the last crevasse or Tim's might not be the only accident they had today.

*OH, YOU'D HAVE known.*

Max glanced over the side and shuddered, quickly averting her eyes. The implication being Tim would have shouted all the way to the bottom if Zach hadn't caught him in time.

Max's stomach cramped and a light sheen of sweat broke out along her upper lip. Moments ago she'd watched Tim and Zach claw their way back on top of the stone bridge, certain that they were both going over. Unadulterated panic was still coursing through her body in an adrenaline dump that left her lightheaded and queasy. However, stark terror was not an image she wanted to project. She knew she needed to walk over and check on Tim, but try as she might she couldn't make her feet move.

She swallowed hard against the ratcheting madness in her system and the throbbing in her temples. She was starting to get the flashing lights around the edges of her vision that signaled an oncoming ocular migraine. Unbelievable. Zach and Michael had enough to deal with without her completely losing it, but Jesus, this was the stuff of her nightmares. She'd be ready for a padded cell once they got topside again.

She could feel Zach's eyes on her. She looked up to meet

his penetrating gaze and realized in that moment she was busted. Something passed between them. He knew she was on the verge of white-hot hysteria and before the day was over, she was going to have to explain herself. That more than anything served as a glass of cold water in the face, helping to spur her on to getting a grip on the emotions that were spiraling out of control.

How was she going to explain herself? The lead scientist for Earth Pharm, heading the expedition into Devil's Hollow, was claustrophobic and basically scared silly of her research venue. Plus she was on the verge of being blind for the next forty-five minutes to an hour. That just made one burst with confidence in the outcome of the project. She reached for her backpack and migraine meds.

When she looked up from peeling the Relpax tablet out of the foil pouch, Zach was towering over her. One minute he'd been a few feet away, now he was crowding her, in her personal space.

At least she assumed it was Zach. She was going strictly by feel now. Her vision was severely limited by the impression of twinkling lights and the cave's darkness. It would be an interesting experience if she didn't know what was to follow—at least three hours of mind-numbing pain.

"You okay?" he asked.

Yeah, it was Zach. She recognized the low, sexy voice. She waited a beat before answering. Her head wasn't hurting yet, like yesterday on the drive with Don. But it would be soon. The greater cause for concern was her rapidly deteriorating vision. Soon she would have to be led by the hand like a blind woman without her cane.

"Shouldn't I be asking you that?" She popped the tablet dry and glanced up after she swallowed.

The light from his headlamp shone in her eyes and the stabbing pain forced her to turn away as he answered. "I'm fine, Max. What's the medicine for?"

She took a silent breath before answering. "I get headaches."

"Sorry to hear that. They stress related?"

"Sometimes. More like migraines."

"Uh-huh. You think it's a good idea to be down in this cave when you're in the middle of a migraine?"

"No, but I didn't really plan on having one."

"Yes, but you had one yesterday. Don told me about those pills on the drive from the airport. You made an impression."

She snorted a tiny laugh. "What every woman wants." She still couldn't face him as she spoke. "Your headlamp is really hurting my eyes."

He reached up to switch off the beam and squatted down beside her. "Sorry, is that better?"

"Thanks, yeah. Um, Zach, look. I appreciate what you did for Tim. I can't tell you how much. I still can't quite believe how fast it happened. You saved his life."

There was an awkward pause as she struggled for words. How to ask him? He didn't fill the silence.

"I've got another problem I need your help with. And I can't let anyone else on the team know about this if it's possible."

"Yeah?" He sounded suspicious.

There was no choice here but to spill it all and hope for the best. "I've got an ophthalmic migraine coming on. Do you know what that is?"

"No." His voice was completely neutral.

"It's basically a migraine in my eyes. I can't see much of anything right now. My vision usually clears within an hour or so."

"What about the pain?"

"The pain's not too bad."

"And after your vision clears?"

"It'll be somewhat intense after that."

"When did this happen?"

"Right after Tim got off the bridge with you and Michael. My head started hurting a little and my vision got distorted. It's sort of like Christmas twinkle lights at the corners of your eyes, then things go gray and then sometimes everything goes black for a while. But with me it's never for more than an hour."

"How often does this happen?" His voice was still neutral.

"I haven't had one in two years. I never had migraines at all and then—" She stopped. She wasn't going there.

He said nothing, so she kept talking. Everything had gone gray within her field of vision. Even the twinkle lights were gone.

"They've tried a little bit of everything to get rid of the regular migraines. So far, rest and lower stress seem to be the best remedies. I haven't had an ocular migraine since those first ones until today."

"And I'm sure you get lots of rest and low stress in your job, right?" There was a little warmth in his voice now.

"Of course, every day." She smiled.

"So what do you want me to do?"

"I don't want you to tell Sal or any of the team about this. They've got enough strikes against the project without worrying that I'm not well enough to be doing the job."

"Won't they realize that something's wrong when we're leading you by the hand out of the cave?"

Inwardly, she cringed at that mental picture. "Well, I was hoping we could come up with a reason for me to stay by myself for a while, until I get my vision back. They know I get migraines, so my staying in tonight at the Lodge won't be an issue. But I need a reason for staying here until I can see to get out on my own."

"Hmm."

"Maybe I could stay here with the equipment until you can come back and get me? We can't leave it, not after what happened earlier, and it will take three of you to carry Tim."

He made another noncommittal sound.

"Over the top, I know, but I'm 'Maximum Maxine.' They'll be expecting it. Besides, I can say I'm taking temperature readings. We didn't do that at the pool and we actually need them from various parts of the cave to see if they vary."

"Except you won't be able to read the thermometer," he reminded her drily.

She didn't answer, and she didn't need her sight to see the skepticism in his face.

"Why should I do this? You've been a pain in the butt since you arrived. You do realize that, don't you?"

She nodded. "But it's only because I really care about doing the job right."

"Risking your health and life for women's makeup?"

After what he'd just done for Tim, Max hated lying. But she had no choice. Explaining everything right here could backfire and he had to help her now. "It's a new financial market Earth Pharm is pursuing. Crucial to its bottom line."

"Of course." His voice chilled considerably. "Are you telling me everything? 'Cause I get the feeling you're leaving something out."

"Well, I should probably tell you that I'm claustrophobic, as well."

"Sweet Jesus. What the hell were they doing putting you in charge of this?"

That stung, particularly as she'd been wondering the same thing herself. "Believe me, you don't want all the gory details."

"Hey, Zach, you got a minute?" Michael called from the direction of the ledge and Tim.

"Sure. Be right there." Zach turned back to her. "Yeah, I do want all the gory details. But now isn't the time. You will tell me everything, and I mean everything, when I come back. Or I'll leave your ass here in the dark. Got it?"

She swallowed audibly and smiled. "Got it. And, Zach, thank you."

"Save the thank-yous for later, Max. You may not be grateful by the time I'm done with you."

ZACH STOOD AND stretched. His back was going to hurt like hell from tackling Tim on the rocks, then stretching himself on the stone bridge as if he were on a medieval rack. Good Lord, how was he going to get these people through this job safely? Between Max's blinding headaches, the scientists' lack of athletic ability and Kirk's refusal to tell him exactly what they were doing here in the first place, he was tempted to chuck the entire project.

But then he wouldn't be able to explore the caves. There had to be a catch for him to get what he wanted and here it was. There was no way the research was about women's makeup. The beautiful scientist was going to get herself killed on his watch. Her story about the headaches was just asinine enough to be true. That was probably the one thing she wasn't lying about.

He popped his back and went over to spin a tale for the scientists as to why they would be leaving Max here in the dark while they carried Tim out. He'd tell Michael what was up if he could get him away from Sal and Tim long enough.

*Jesus. What a disaster.*

MAX LISTENED TO the men walk away in the darkness. On Zach's advice she turned off her headlamp to conserve the batteries for when he got back and the light would actually be useful. The dull glow that had been shining a few feet ahead of her disappeared and stygian blackness closed in. The twinkle lights had long since passed. She closed her eyes, hoping the sensation of pressure and tightness would pass.

No good.

She took deep breaths. Shallow breaths. Quick sips of air.

Still she felt the flutters of a panic attack beating against her tightening chest and throat from far away. She reached up and switched on the headlamp.

Nothing happened. No comforting glow. She flipped the switch again.

Still nothing.

She fumbled in the darkness and rapidly turned the switch a multitude of times. Nada.

Slipping the helmet off her head, she shook the LED lantern hoping to reconnect some misaligned wiring.

Utter blackness.

Hot prickles of sweat dotted her upper lip as she battled the urge to scream, to call out for the men to come back. She couldn't do this. Couldn't face her demons in the dark.

They were too old, too powerful. Too ingrained. She hadn't slept with the lights on since her senior year in high school, but still...

Flashbacks to childhood. A tiny closet in a cabin. A locked door. A horrible summer at an all-girls' camp when her mother was first diagnosed and away in the hospital. Crying in the dark when the counselors were out smoking cigarettes and not watching their charges.

*"Let me out, please. Someone, let me out."*

Laughter from the other girls in her cabin, but no one opening the door.

She shook the lamp again. "Come on, damn it." She twisted the switch back and forth and bopped the whole mechanism lightly with her hand. Magically it lit. A dull glow with her limited vision, but she was able to breathe again. Abruptly the glow disappeared with an electrical popping sound.

*Crap.* She tapped it on the ground this time. Once. Twice. Something shattered. Had to be the bulb. She put her hand on the front of the lamp. A sharp edge nicked her finger. She sucked on the cut spot and tasted the metallic tang of blood.

She sat very still for a moment, despair and fear welling inside. Hot tears pricked at the corners of her eyes. Her heart rate increased steadily. She had to hold it together. She took a shuddering breath and tried humming a bit. She might sound like a deranged yoga instructor, but at this point she was willing to try anything.

She wasn't sure how long she crooned a soft monotone; eventually she was able to fashion a tune. More of a scale. Her pulse slowed to barely jumping through her skin so she could think beyond the paralyzing fear that had been present earlier.

She had some fast figuring to do. Zach was going to want answers to questions she wasn't allowed to even acknowledge, according to Kirk. But she couldn't stand lying anymore after everything he'd done for her and the team today.

She leaned her head back against the wall of rock and clasped her hands around her knees. The suffocating darkness pressed down. She tried not to think about it; she'd hyperventilate if she did. She wished she could sleep, but that was impossible. She was cold and stiff, so she tried moving around a bit without putting her hands on the ground where the pieces of broken headlamp were. Her boots made scraping noises on the cavern floor, and she had to sweep away something sharp from under her butt.

In the darkness her senses were heightened. In the stillness she could hear the stream below the natural bridge. She didn't allow herself to think about rising floodwaters. Instead she focused on the smell of mold and dampness, the scent of minerals in the air. And finally, from a distance she heard the distinct sound of footsteps.

Either Zach was coming or a very large bat. God, she didn't want to even think about the creatures that were in here with her. She'd just gotten her blood pressure under control.

The clomping of footsteps grew louder. She hoped it was Zach.

Or the people who'd tampered with their equipment?

Her supersensitized hearing picked up the sound of metal rasping against rock over the sound of the running water. She tamped down the fear and started humming again.

## Chapter Eight

Bathed in a dim yellow glow, Max could smell the tangy scent of man and sweat as Zach leaned over her.

"Max, how you doing?" His low voice was soothing to her jangled nerves. Then he was touching her face. "You okay?" His fingers were warm on her cheek. "Hey, you were crying."

"I was?" She hadn't realized it. "I'm okay. Really."

"Hmm." The glow was suddenly brighter as he shone the light directly in her face. This time she was able to see more clearly than before. It hurt just as much, too.

"I'm okay. Really. I was just…"

"Frightened?"

*Scared spitless.* "Reliving some of life's more difficult moments." She tried to smile, but felt her jaw tighten in a grimace.

"Well, that'll drive you crazy. Sitting here by yourself in the dark."

"Thanks for the warning."

He reached out a hand to help her up. "Let's go. Turn on your light."

"It's broken."

"What?"

She explained, ending with, "Sometimes I'm not very patient."

"I'll remember that. I've got a slip-on headlamp for emergencies that fits like a sweatband. Do you think it will make your headache worse?" He hadn't let go of her hand yet.

"I don't think so. My head's doing pretty good, unless you shine a light directly in my eyes."

"Sorry." He dropped her hand and started digging in his pack. "How's Tim?"

"Knocked out on Demerol for now and on his way to the hospital. Michael and Don took everyone back, so it's just you and me." He slid the headband around her forehead and switched on the light.

"How's that?"

She gingerly moved her chin up and down. "It's 'kay." She was surprised. Normally her head would be pounding mercilessly at this point, but her migraines had always been different from the norm.

He took her hand again and helped her stand, leading her beside him. The warmth of his hand was a welcome relief after her freak-out there in the dark. "You said you gave Tim Demerol? You have really good drugs."

He laughed. "I have EMT certification along with the park ranger training. I think that's part of why Kirk wants me here. Michael and I have an excellent first-aid kit in the truck."

"Thank you for taking care of Tim. I still can't believe how fast this happened." They were crossing the last natural bridge. She hesitated and felt herself tense up. He squeezed her hand and she took a deep breath before creeping forward.

"Yeah, well, that's the nature of accidents. They happen quick...otherwise they'd be called planned events."

She didn't say anything. She was focused on breathing and not hyperventilating until they'd gotten beyond the bridge.

"What's your team doing here, Max?"

The question was so unexpected, she stopped walking, caught off guard. She peered at him through the darkness. Her eyes were adjusting to the light and no longer ached like they had before. The ocular part of her headache was past and the bridge was behind her. She felt stronger. "You realize I'm not allowed to say." She dropped his hand and immediately missed the warmth it had provided.

"I know that's the bullshit story you've been told to tell me once your back is to the wall, but that's not gonna fly this time. I need to know what the hell is going on. The sabotage this morning. The councilmen at the Lodge. This isn't some ordinary research project. I'd like to know what's going on before I'm required to go over a ledge again."

"You've been hired to do a job. Why does it matter what the project is?"

"Max, you're smarter than that. This isn't the Secret Service. And I'm not laying down my life for the president. I want to know what I'm risking my neck for or I might not be as willing to leap next time. I'm sure as hell not doing it so women can have a dewy complexion in any light."

For a moment she was taken aback, then she realized he was right, even if he was misquoting a famous cosmetics advertising slogan. It wasn't fair to ask him to risk his life when he had no idea what the project was about.

She took a deep breath. The walls of the cavern were closing in again. "Not here, okay? I'll explain everything topside, but I can't talk about it now."

"You stalling?"

"No. Hand to God. I just want to get out of here."

He looked at her long and hard. She couldn't see his eyes in the glare of the headlamp he was wearing.

"All right, but we're not done," he said.

"Agreed. We're not done."

"Were you going to tell me you had claustrophobia?"

"Not unless it came up," she admitted.

"Consider the subject raised."

"When we get out of here, okay?"

"Oh, yeah. I wanna hear it all," he said.

Weaving their way out of the cavern in relative silence, Max focused on breathing again and not tripping or slipping on the damp, uneven floor on her way to the vertical entry/exit chamber. On her hands and knees in the tunnel, the rough walls of the cave changed to smooth flowstone halfway through her long crawl. The loose muddy gravel on the floor became one slick piece of flat rock. For once her claustrophobia didn't bother her. Perhaps because she knew she was almost home. On the other end, Zach clipped her into the ascender and belayed her to the surface.

Finally Max was standing above ground in the open air. She didn't kneel down to kiss the dirt, but the thought crossed her mind. Zach didn't seem to notice her giddy relief at being out of the cave. He was busy coiling the lines and stowing the climbing gear in bags.

The salvaged lab equipment was gone except for one bag. She unzipped the duffel, postponing the inevitable.

How was she going to tell Zach? He would want to know it all. He deserved to know everything. How did she do this and keep her word to Kirk?

Torn, she had no idea. But she'd never been a coward.

Max zipped the duffel and carried it to the bed of the pickup. "It's cancer research," she blurted.

If he was surprised at her outburst, he didn't show it. "What kind of cancer research?"

"A possible 'cancer-eating' drug."

He set his bags down beside hers in the truck bed and leaned against the tailgate. "Tell me about it."

"In Ellen Garrett's experiment, the bacteria in the pond ate cancer cells and leaft healthy tissue behind."

He waited a beat. "Damn." He shook his head. "Amazing."

That was the reaction she'd been waiting for. "Right. It's rather remarkable."

"It's unbelievable," he said.

"Yes, it is."

"Wait a minute. Do you believe it's true?"

"What do you mean?" she asked.

"Do you honestly believe that kind of fantastical story could be true?"

Max studied the sky and felt the first spurt of anger since she'd gotten above ground. The sun was just starting to set. Pinks, blues, purples and oranges melded across the sky in a spectacular display. Striving to compose her emotions, she coolly turned from nature's art show to face him.

"Ellen's experiment provided the first building block. We're here to see if we can reproduce the results inside the cave, then see if we can duplicate them outside the cave."

"Okay, I notice you didn't answer my question. But we'll get back to that. Why the two venues?"

She swallowed the angry retort and imagined herself an iceberg. "A couple of reasons. And maybe this will answer your question. Inside the cave, to see if the whole thing is true. Outside to see if it's transferable. Plus there's a small situation with the lease."

"Ah, yes, Farmer Tillman."

Max nodded.

"How long is your lease?"

"Six weeks. We have to be able to produce this outside the cavern in case he decides not to extend our access. We'd like to buy the land, but we have to keep it secret so our competitors don't find out about it and buy it out from under us. Earth Pharm can't afford to get into a bidding war over this."

"I just bet they can't." The bitterness in his tone was palpable and Max didn't understand it.

The sun dipped toward the horizon.

"It'll be dark soon. You have anything else you need to grab? With all the rain this month, it'll get buggy quick. Trust me, that 'everything's bigger in Texas' adage applies to mosquitoes. We want to get out of here before they arrive."

Max didn't need any more convincing than that. Her

phobia of bugs and the great outdoors overrode her frustration with Zach. She hopped into the passenger seat and fastened her seat belt while he gathered the last of his climbing equipment. She watched him in the side mirror.

The leather seats were warm from the day's heat. The truck smelled like him. Being this close to him in the dying light wasn't going to be a good thing. She felt lethargic and had the sensation of being drugged or having had too much wine. Lost inhibitions.

When he climbed into the driver's seat, instantly she felt surrounded in the semidarkness. Only this time she wasn't suffocating, she was aroused.

What the hell was going on with her? She was supposed to be "off men," particularly this one. Hadn't her experience with Robert, the rat bastard, taught her anything?

She glanced at Zach's chiseled profile in the glow of the dying sunset. Well, Robert hadn't looked like that.

Zach glanced at her as he put the keys in the ignition and suddenly everything the guy was doing seemed erotic. Why she had no idea. He must be piping some kind of aphrodisiac air into his truck, because she was ready to rip the man's clothes off.

"You ready to go?"

She cleared her throat and desperately reached out for the most unerotic thing she could think of to clear her head.

Replacing her pilfered Toby jugs on eBay. Okay, that was very nonsexy.

"Um, yeah. Yeah, I am." She focused on his hand turning the ignition key and wondered what his fingers would feel like on her—

"Max?"

"Yes?"

"I asked if you wanted to go to the hospital to check on Tim."

"Ah…yes." How long had she been staring at his hands imagining them on her body? "Yes, that would be great. I'd like that." What was wrong with her? She was grateful for the wash of the red sunset as she felt the blush working its way from the top of her head to her toes.

"He may be asleep."

"That's okay. I need to check on him to give a report to Kirk anyway."

"Whatever you say. How's your head?" He put the truck in Drive and started down the incline.

"Good, great in fact. I can't quite believe it. Normally I'm toast after one of those headaches, but not today. I guess caves are good for migraines somehow." Max laughed, but it came out sounding high-pitched and nervous. And she didn't get nervous around men. She kept her eyes firmly on the dirt track road.

"So you gonna tell me about that claustrophobia now?"

Oh God, not now. She wasn't sure she could. Not when she was drowning in thoughts of how she'd like to do him on the bench seat of his truck.

"Ah, no, not really."

"Wrong answer."

"Yeah, kind of figured you would say that." The easiest way to do this was going to be fast. Like yanking off a bandage. Plus she'd hit on the most unerotic thing to think about.

"It's not anything awful. I didn't have a wicked stepfather or anything horrible like that. Just a horrid experience at a summer camp."

He didn't talk, but he stopped in the middle of the dirt road as she did. *Great.* He wasn't going to let her just spill her guts as he drove. He was going to study her as she eviscerated herself with painful memories.

She took a steadying breath and turned to face him head-on, the way she'd learned to deal with this particular incident. "I was at summer camp and the girls in my cabin all knew each other. They thought it great sport to lock me in the broom closet at night while the counselors were out smoking cigarettes and meeting their boyfriends."

"How long did this go on?"

"All summer. No one knew about it and I didn't tell."

"Why not?" His hands clenched hard on the steering wheel. She could see his knuckles in the light from the dashboard.

"My mother had just been diagnosed with cancer and was having a stem-cell transplant while I was away at camp. I worried that if I told anyone, she'd stop the transplant, come get me and maybe die. So I stayed quiet."

"My God. How old were you?"

"Nine."

"Jesus. Kids can be cruel."

"It wasn't that bad."

"Sure. You just can't handle being in the dark without flipping out."

"That's not true."

"Yeah? So you weren't about to jump out of your skin when I came back to get you in the cave?" He wasn't wearing a seat belt and slid across to the middle of the bench seat as he spoke.

She knew he was right, but it still ticked her off. She dropped her head and sighed heavily. "Well, yeah. I might have had a hard time today. But that was different." She lifted her eyes to meet his. "Extenuating circumstances."

He sat so close she could feel the heat from his body. Could see the intensity of his gaze with just the glow of the dashboard.

"What kind of extenuating circumstances?" he asked.

Her breath caught as she stared into his green eyes. She was going to kiss him and it was going to be incredible and damn it, she might be making a huge mistake, but she didn't care. She just wanted to feel this man's hands, lips, everything on her body. Right now.

"These." She leaned forward and he met her halfway, tunneling his hands into her hair a split second after their lips met.

Max had never been much for grading kissers. Maybe because she hadn't been with many guys who were particularly skilled in the art. Zach blew their curve out of the water.

The kiss was hot, wet and filled with the promise that he could deliver some other mind-blowing delights, as well.

Coming up for air, she was shaken by that intensity. She pulled herself back from his embrace and put up a hand when he would have pulled her back into his arms. "You are slightly dangerous," she said.

He merely raised an eyebrow. "That might be mutual."

Max shook her head. "I think I'm in serious trouble here."

"I don't know if I'd call it trouble." He leaned in and kissed her again, softly this time, running his hand from her shoulder to her waist.

She started to tense up, but Zach deepened the kiss as he reached beside her hip to unlock her seat belt and brush the buckle away.

Against her better judgment, she edged closer to him on the bench seat. Just one more kiss.

He slid his arm around her and pulled her toward him. They were hip to knee beside each other, but that wasn't close enough. She bent her neck for better access to his lips. Running her hands across his chest, she felt the soft cotton of his shirt. It was dusty and dirty. They were both covered in cave grit, but she didn't care.

The temperature seemed to rise in the cab of the truck. Without breaking the kiss, he put his hands on either side of her waist and picked her up, placing her over his hips to straddle him on the seat.

She felt heat and the hardness of him between her thighs and she wanted. Oh, she wanted him. Here. Now.

He reached between them for the button of her jeans and some alarm in the back of her head started jangling, but she ignored it. Ignored everything, forgetting why this had seemed like a bad idea earlier. He slid a hand down the front of her jeans past her cotton panties and her mind completely disconnected from her body.

He whispered in her ear. "Max, tell me what you want. Exactly what you want."

She struggled to find her voice and finally said, "This. I want this. And everything else. You inside me."

She felt his smile against her check as he kissed her. "That can be arranged."

The feel of the words against her ear along with what he was doing with his fingers combined to send her over the edge and shatter into a thousand shimmering pieces.

She wasn't sure but she might have screamed.

He held her loosely with one arm and kept caressing her with those clever fingers as he kissed her back to some semblance of consciousness. Surprisingly, he didn't ask for anything in return.

But she didn't want to leave things halfway done for him. She pulled at his jeans and briefs, getting them past his hips as she tugged and pulled. When she would have taken him in her hands, he grabbed her wrists.

"I'm not someone you can just 'do' and get out of your system, Max. And I'm not here to scratch your itch. No matter how quickly we got here."

She looked into his eyes. They had an odd luminescence either from the light of the dash or the dying sun. She was taken aback by the ferocity she saw there. "Fair warning, no one likes being used."

"I'm not using you. I want this," she said.

"Obviously, I do, too."

He reached into his jeans pocket for his wallet and came up with a slightly wrinkled package.

A condom. Thank God, even ex-park rangers were always prepared. She felt a tiny giggle bubble up inside, more from nerves and relief that he had a condom. She wasn't stupid enough to go forward without one at this point, no matter how caught up she was in the moment.

That gave her pause but not for long, because he was pulling and tugging at her jeans and soon they were both as close to naked as they needed to be. She helped him get the condom in place, then he was lifting her up again and studying her face. "Is this what you really want?" he asked.

She looked down at the impressive dimensions before her.

"Oh yeah, this is definitely what I wan—"

He'd just been waiting for her *yes*. Before she finished speaking, he was deep inside her and she could only gasp at the sensation. She was stretching and he was very still as she gazed into his eyes in utter amazement.

"Breathe, Max. Just breathe," he whispered.

She nodded slowly and he began to move beneath her. She felt the friction of him against herself, felt the tension building again.

When she would have looked away, Zach gently held her chin with his thumb and forefinger. The intimacy of staring into his green eyes as they both slowly built to orgasm was overwhelming. Still, she closed her eyes in the final moments and hugged him to her chest, ironically unable to reveal herself laid that bare by looking into his face.

Afterward, Max untangled herself almost immediately. And Zach took his cue well. He didn't say anything and he didn't try to hold her. Instead he reached under the seat and handed her a half-liter of bottled water.

"Do you need this?" His voice was a whisper, but it seemed extraordinarily loud after what had just passed between them.

Max felt that horrid blush again. "Thanks," she muttered, as she shimmied into her jeans.

Feeling very much like a crab, she grabbed the water and hopped out of the truck. It was full dark, but right now she didn't care about mosquitoes or any other bugs. She had to get out of the vehicle and away from him for a minute to clear her head. Everything in that truck smelled like Zach and sex.

What had she been thinking? Well, that was obvious. She hadn't. She'd been horny and scratching an itch. Exactly what Zach had asked her not to do.

She scrambled to the tailgate, cleaned herself up as best she could, and got a couple of mosquito bites in unfortunate places in the process. She made her way to the cab door in record time and slammed inside. He glanced at her once to make sure she was situated before starting the engine.

"I, um…I don't usually do this," mumbled Max.

"I gathered that."

"Well, I'm sure you have more experi—" She stopped. That was totally the wrong thing to say.

He didn't answer for a moment, but when he did his voice was arctic. "What are you saying, Max? You think I make a habit of nailing every woman who sits in the passenger seat of my truck? Or do you just think this was a mistake?"

She turned to him because, in the face of those words, she had to. "I don't believe we were thinking at all. That's the problem. I don't know what you usually do and I don't care."

"Sure you do, Max." If possible his voice grew cooler with each syllable. "You have a problem with losing control." He leaned toward her for the first time since he'd set her back on the seat. "And let me tell you, sweetheart. You lost all control there for a while."

It was like having a bucket of ice water dumped on her head. "That's a horrible thing to say." *Even if it is true.* "Look, I don't think it was a mistake, because the sex was extraordinarily hot, but the timing is abysmal. I can't do this right now. I just broke off an engagement and I'm in charge of this project."

"I'm not looking for a relationship, Max."

"So neither of us are in a good place for this?"

He snorted a laugh. "Hell, no."

"So you think it was a mistake?" she asked. She didn't know why she was pressing the issue so, only that she had to.

He shook his head. "Okay, if it'll make you feel better to call it that. We made an error in judgment. Don't worry, though. I don't kiss and tell."

An unreasonable sense of relief washed over her. "So, this—" she waved her hand at the cab "—never happened."

"Whatever you say, Dr. O'Neil."

IN A PIG'S friggin' eye. There was no way Zach could pretend this had never happened. And some part of him was wondering why. Why was this woman getting to him so? He'd just met her yesterday. He should be able to enjoy the hot sex and forget about the rest.

That was easier said than done. He couldn't ignore her or forget about it. Sex with Max was anything but uncomplicated. Especially not now, when he couldn't take a breath without smelling her. How in holy hell had this happened? One minute they'd been sitting there talking about her childhood phobias of the dark and the next minute he'd been inside her.

Having sex wasn't a mistake, but he didn't know what to call it.

She'd lied to him about Earth Pharm's research. He wasn't positive he had the whole story even now. A cancer-eating bacteria? It hardly seemed possible. The one thing he was sure of was that he couldn't believe what she told him. And he couldn't ignore the effect she had on him, either.

They drove in silence for fifteen minutes.

Max was licking her wounds, hostility pouring off her. Zach didn't even have to be a Dr. Phil fan to pick up on that. He knew he hadn't been kind. But he was still smarting from her words, as well.

As the silence lingered, he realized he had to say something—anything—to change the focus from what had just happened or their working situation would be impossible.

"So about this research you're doing for Earth Pharm. Do you honestly believe it's real? A cancer-eating drug?"

"Of course. Why wouldn't I?" She still sounded defensive, but at least now the conversation was aimed toward her work and not at him.

"Oh, I don't know. Something about it sounds too good to be true."

"I believe Ellen Garrett's research is true and I believe in Earth Pharm's initial evaluation of that data."

"I see." He tried to keep the skepticism out of his tone, but didn't do a very good job.

"Who do you think I shouldn't be trusting?" she asked.

"Well, I'm not a big fan of pharmaceutical companies of any kind."

"But you're working for one."

"Yes, but it's because I want into Devil's Hollow. The means to an end."

"I suppose that's very pragmatic of you. Why are you not a fan?"

He took a moment before answering. He wasn't sure he wanted to go here, then decided to hell with it. He'd already made so many colossal mistakes with this woman tonight, there didn't appear to be much hope for redemption.

"A pharmaceutical company murdered my sister."

# Chapter Nine

*Telling her might have been a mistake.* Zach didn't look at Max after he spoke. A jackrabbit dashed across the road in the headlights' glare and he drove a half mile before she said anything.

"I don't mean to pry, but could you please explain that?" she asked.

"Do you remember the PharmaVax scandal earlier this year?" His eyes never left the road.

"You mean about the senator who exchanged favorable vaccine policy for campaign contributions? Sure. PharmaVax was my old company. I was very interested."

He nodded in the darkness. "You may recall that several people were murdered. One of them was Tammy Douglas. She was my twin sister."

"Oh, Zach. I'm…I'm sorry." She paused a beat. "Michael mentioned something to me about this."

Zach smiled grimly. "Warned you about it, most likely." He drove on in silence for a moment. "Tammy was in the wrong place at the wrong time and they killed her for it."

"Do you think Earth Pharm is like PharmaVax?"

Something clicked inside when she asked the question and he didn't answer at first. He knew a flaw had been exposed in his argument, but he wasn't willing to examine it. He had too much invested in his belief.

"Yes, I do. I think everyone is lying on some level, if not overtly, then to themselves about what they're doing working for the pharmaceutical industry."

"I'm sorry you feel that way," said Max.

"I don't think it's all pernicious, but I believe some folks who work for the industry are being lied to."

"Me included?"

That was a loaded question that he wasn't sure how to answer. The point of this whole conversation had been to get her not to be so mad at him. His silence was louder than words. He had to say something.

"There's nothing malicious about what you're doing here. I think you believe in your project. But I also think it's a...pipe dream." He knew that was the wrong thing to say even as the words left his lips.

"Oh, so you don't think I'm being used. Only misled. Whew. What a relief. I'm just naive." Her voice was sharp. She was ticked and didn't care if he knew it. "No one likes being called a fool, Zach, even an unintentional one."

"I'm not calling you a fool. But I don't like your employer."

"News flash, Zach. It's *your* employer, too."

He laughed. "Yeah, and don't I know it. A necessary evil for what I want."

"And what is it you want so badly that you would deign to work for Earth Pharm?"

He didn't know if he should answer, then decided he might as well. He could hardly say anything to upset her more than she already was. "I want to survey the cavern."

"Why?"

"I discovered it along with Michael and Ellen the day Tammy died and—God, how do I describe this? I've been looking for a cave like that my entire life. I went home the day we broke through the entry tunnel to bury my sister. When I got back, Earth Pharm was here. So, yes, your company is very much a necessary evil."

He could feel her studying him even through the darkness. "I think I can understand why you feel that way," she said.

He wasn't sure if he wanted her to understand him or not. They rode in silence for a mile. "What about you?" he asked. "What are you doing here? There's no way you can convince me that you belong in this environment."

"It's the project of a lifetime. I jumped at the opportunity when Kirk offered me the spot on the team."

He nodded. "Okay, so I've got to ask, and yeah, it's none of my business, but who is Kirk to you? Did I just have sex with my boss's girlfriend?"

Max laughed out loud. The first genuine belly laugh he'd heard from her since they'd met.

"No, Ralph Kirk isn't my lover. He was my best friend's father in college. Because both my parents were gone, I spent summers and holidays with Mallory and her folks. They became my family. Two weeks before graduation Mallory and her mom were killed in a car accident. Kirk was devastated and I was, too. We were the only family the other had left. So he basically adopted me. Nothing legal. Just…he's like my dad, but not really."

*Oh, great.* "Adopted fathers tend to carry weapons where their daughters are concerned."

He heard the smile in her voice again. "In this case, I don't think so." They drew closer to town as she talked. "But in all seriousness, while you may believe it's a lie, for me the Devil's Hollow project is huge. The biggest project I've ever had the opportunity to work on. And I know Kirk would never lie to me about it."

"I think you're very trusting," said Zach.

"I'm going to have to be to counter your cynicism."

He shook his head. "I prefer to think of it as realism." Zach pulled into the hospital lot and found a spot to park.

"No matter what you want to call it, I can't blow this project. That's why I'm not sure this is the best time for me to have a hot affair with you. We're talking about cancer research that could bring about a cure. Do you realize how big that is?"

The beam from the mercury vapor light overhead shone into the cab, illuminating her face. His eyes never wavered from hers. She was all sincerity and concern and he was falling into her like he had when they'd been making love earlier. He wanted her and he was irritated with her at the same time.

He had to stop this now or he was going to be lost in something he wasn't ready for. He took a mental step back.

"Sure, I understand the ramifications, but I don't believe in the tooth fairy or the Easter bunny. And I don't believe you have a cure for cancer in that cave. I do believe in cold, hard, cash, though, and getting into that cavern for my own benefit. As for the other…" He shrugged.

"Don't sweat the hot affair stuff, Max. I won't out you in front of your team. They'll never know about us unless you tell them. I was hired to protect you and your people in the caverns. I'll do that. And I'll keep my hands off you from now on if that's what you prefer." He finished with a lazy smile, but his chest was tight.

Her face blanched and her eyes widened. He knew he'd been an ass, but it was necessary for his sanity. He'd do the job he'd been hired to do and nothing else from now on. No sex on the side.

My God, what had he been thinking? The woman had lied to him and worked for a pharmaceutical company just like PharmaVax. She used to actually work *for* PharmaVax. Tammy's murderer. It was just wrong on so many levels, no matter how casual.

Clearing her throat, she regarded the parking lot before fixing him with her blue gaze. "I believe that would be best."

*Perfect.* "Let's go check on Tim."

MAX RAN THROUGH the rain ahead of Zach only because she knew the quicker she got inside, the sooner she'd be alone.

She was exhausted but so relieved to be back at the Lodge, she wanted to weep. Mentally she was toast. The time in the cave, the sex, the conversation with Zach and then the doctors and staff they'd dealt with at the hospital had done her in. If Max couldn't take a shower soon she was going to be a raving lunatic.

The good thing was they'd left Tim resting well. He had a broken ankle and two cracked ribs, but overall the lab scientist was damn lucky to be alive.

A blue Mercedes blocked her path to the porch steps. Certainly not one of the team members' cars. She didn't want to think about who had ridden out to Whispering Pines in the rising storm. It didn't bode well. With Zach on her heels, she jogged around the luxury vehicle that had seen better days and dashed through the drizzling rain.

He stopped her at the oak-paneled door and she searched his face in the glow of the porch's yellow bug light. The bulb cast an odd shadow on his eyes and she couldn't read the expression there. She was afraid he was going to bring up what had happened back in his truck and she just couldn't. Not now. All she wanted was to get inside, out of the great outdoors and into a hot shower, find something to eat and— God, she'd give a week's pay for a glass of merlot.

As she reached for the wrought-iron handle, Zach gently slid his hand past her wrist and opened the heavy door himself. She turned toward him and his arm brushed the side of her breast. The contact was unexpected. Electric. He was so close she could feel the warmth of his breath on her temple. She stared with what had to be a comical expression and swallowed hard. "Yes?"

"I'm just opening the door."

She eyed him nervously. "I can do it myself." She pulled her hand back anyway. "I don't understand what you want. Please don't play games with me. I can't deal with that right now." *I may be acting like a coward, but I can't help myself.* Emotionally, she was fried.

He shook his head. "I'm not playing games. Max, haven't you ever let anyone open a door for you?"

Without another word, he stepped back, but gave her a scorching look as he pushed the massive door open. There was no time to answer. Mrs. Mabry stood in the entryway with the aroma of brewing coffee and baking cookies wafting toward them.

"Good evening, Zach, Dr. O'Neil. I'm glad you're back before the weather hit hard. There's a man from the newspaper here to see you. Are you just coming from the caverns?"

The change was so abrupt from the spell he'd been weaving around her that Max almost had to shake her head. She physically sagged at the news of visitors. She couldn't deal with any of it until she'd at least washed her face.

Zach answered for them both. "No, ma'am, we stopped by the hospital to check on Tim Ryan first."

"Oh, I was so sorry to hear about the accident. The other team members told me about it. How is Mr. Ryan?"

Max cleared away the fog and answered, "He's going to be okay. I think he'll be in the hospital until we can arrange transport back to New York. He's on some heavy-duty painkillers. He was incredibly lucky."

"I'm glad to hear it. I've got some dinner for you when you're ready or I can bring up a tray if you'd rather. Meanwhile, your guest is in the front living room having some coffee."

"I wasn't expecting anyone."

"I believe he's from *The Reddington County Herald*."

Max groaned inwardly. Newspapers, her worst nightmare. She was a scientist, not Earth Pharm's public relations spokesperson.

They'd been gone for twelve hours and right now she wanted a shower so desperately her teeth hurt. She felt gritty, dirty and smelled of the cave, outdoors and sex. Her head was beating a slight tattoo at the base of her skull, but surprisingly it was nothing like she'd normally expect after one of her "ocular incidents."

"I'll be right there," she told Zach. "I've got to go to the ladies' room first."

She left Zach in the hall and went to the powder room. After taking one look in the mirror, she wished she hadn't. She looked worse than she'd thought. After fixing herself up as best she could, she called it a done deal and went to the parlor.

A man dressed in business attire offered his hand. "Hello, Dr. O'Neil. I'm Carl Madden from *The Reddington County Herald*. I understand you met with several members of the Reddington town council today."

"Yes, I did." Max shook his clammy hand and decided she wasn't going to give him any more than that. He would set the agenda.

"I hear it didn't go too well. I'd like to have your side of the story. For starters I'd like to understand, as would our readers, why Earth Pharm refuses to open the cavern to tourism. What is it exactly that you are researching down there?"

Max dredged up a smile that she hoped looked sincere. "I'm so sorry that you made the trip out here to Whispering Pines for this question. As I explained to the councilmen earlier, we're researching a new mineral for women's makeup. I'm not at liberty to discuss the details of our work. We are a privately held company and develop competitive products for the open market. I hope you understand my position."

Carl was shaking his head. "I'm afraid I don't."

With a superhuman effort, Max gritted her teeth and smiled again instead of sighing. "If you had a new invention for harvesting corn, you wouldn't announce it to the world before you had a patent, would you? Your competitors might beat you to the punch. No?"

"Perhaps. But don't the residents of Reddington have a right to know why they are being denied this economic boon by a large pharmaceutical company?"

Max realized she'd just heard the headline for Madden's

story. There wasn't any way to combat that kind of blind prejudice. Even with the truth.

She smiled again, clenching her jaw so hard she was sure to crack a molar. "I understand your point. Do you understand that what you're asking could destroy the reason for our being here? The cave's ecosystem might not be able to take that kind of intrusion. If that's the case, what we're studying would be useless."

"But don't people have the right to judge for themselves?"

The tenuous hold began to slip on her temper. He hadn't been listening to anything she'd said. "Certainly. After they understand all the facts."

He raised an eyebrow. "The facts? All right, the facts. Are you mining diamonds at Devil's Hollow?"

"What? Where is this idea coming from? I assure you, Mr. Madden, we are not mining diamonds at Devil's Hollow."

"You're positive?"

"Yes, I'm positive. That's impossible given the formations of the cave. But the town will be killing the goose that laid the golden egg if the city fathers insist on opening Devil's Hollow before our research is done." She could hear the sarcasm in her voice even as she felt Zach's hand on the small of her back trying to calm her. Unfortunately, she was too far gone at this point to slow down.

"I'm not sure your competitors would feel the same way about it," said Carl.

"Other scientists feel exactly the same way about protecting the cave's ecosystem."

He didn't answer.

"I can't stress this enough. That 'economic boon' you're touting could be ruined by one false misstep in the cavern. That's why we are keeping it closed and under guard until our work here is done."

Madden nodded. "Yes, but it's an open market. What if your competitors could offer more generous terms in their research efforts? The city fathers would be more likely to sell the land to them, no?"

"What are you talking about? Our lease is with Paul Tillman. He owns the land."

"That's debatable right now. Apparently Mr. Tillman just filed for bankruptcy today. He owes the city a significant amount of money in back taxes. Want to guess how much the land Devil's Hollow sits on is worth? I have the numbers right here fresh from the county appraiser." Madden patted his briefcase. "Tillman may be forfeiting that land to the city."

Max's head was spinning. "What?"

"I'm sure Judge Parker will be fair. There's a bankruptcy hearing scheduled for Friday morning. Parker will decide then who has access to the cavern." He leaned back in his chair. "That's one good thing about small-town courts. Fast action for civic situations."

Max saw red. "Sir, that's illegal as hell. You know it and I know it. Forcing our hand will do nothing but tie up the city in a long court battle. If the community is as economically depressed as you say, do they want to do that?"

"If this research is as important as you say, do you want to do that?" asked Madden.

"What does the city really want?"

"Obviously, immediate access to the cave."

"Haven't you been listening? That's impossible. Immediate access will destroy the very thing we're here to research," said Max.

"Yeah, yeah. Killing the goose that laid the golden egg. I got it."

"You got it, all right, Mr. Madden. You're an idiot."

Carl Madden didn't react well to this slur on his intelligence. The interview was over. Max wished she'd known the magic words to make him leave ten minutes earlier.

The newspaperman avoided her completely as he stomped toward the front door. On the way out he stopped and spoke with

Zach in hushed tones. It hadn't occurred to her until now that they might know each other from living in the same community.

Zach nodded his head and muttered, "No, but thank you."

"You've got your work cut out for you, Zach," Madden murmured and walked away without a backward glance.

Max headed toward a wing chair by the fireplace. "Well, that went well," she muttered.

"You have quite a way with the press."

"Oh, shut up," she snapped. "Kirk is going to stroke out over this." She eased into the chair and got comfortable.

"You might want to wait on that," Zach said. "Once you sit, you'll never get up again."

For some reason, being told not to sit down was the last straw. Her anger, simmering for an hour, hit high boil and overflowed its bounds—all over Zach.

"I'm sick of being told what to do," she hissed and plopped her feet on the footstool. Belligerent, she refused to make eye contact with him as Mrs. Mabry bustled in.

"Suit yourself, Max," he said under his breath.

"There's a package for you in your room, Dr. O'Neil."

Max nodded, still fuming.

Mrs. Mabry prattled on, seemingly unaware of the rising tension that could be cut with one of her fine kitchen blades. "You want to eat now or get cleaned up first? I can bring your tray up to you. You look exhausted."

For some reason, Mrs. Mabry's observation didn't bother her. If anything, it defused her anger. "I've got to shower to feel human again. It'll take me ten minutes at the most. But I'll come down to eat."

"Suit yourself, dear. Call down if you change your mind."

Zach snorted a laugh. "Oh, she will."

Mrs. Mabry focused directly on him and totally dispelled Max's earlier notion. "There's nothing wrong with a woman knowing her own mind. It's a rather underestimated value these days."

Max refused to look at Zach. She would smirk or do something equally childish if she did and she'd been childish enough already this evening. Instead, with muscles protesting, she hauled herself out of the chair. She still hated that he'd been right. But if she could make it upstairs without whimpering it would be a major victory.

"I'll be down in ten minutes." She had to because she'd been so snotty and now she knew her own mind. She could have hugged Mrs. Mabry for those encouraging words, but as friendly as the woman appeared, she wasn't the "huggy" type any more than Max was.

Max dragged herself up the stairs and crawled into the shower. The hot water felt indescribably wonderful and revived her mood. Amazingly her head wasn't hurting.

Maybe she'd found the key to controlling her migraines.

Sex.

Well, wasn't that terrific. She had to choose between a big headache—literally or figuratively.

Not that Zach hadn't been amazing. It was the aftermath that was so difficult to navigate. She might as well have been stumbling around in the dark.

She dried off with another threadbare towel, but this one was at least big enough to wrap around her sarong style. She hurried into the bedroom and snagged the mail Mrs. Mabry had mentioned.

One large padded envelope from Earth Pharm and one regular business envelope. The business envelope had no return address and what appeared to be a local postmark. She glanced at the clock. She was hungry, but curiosity won out. Besides Earth Pharm, who knew she was here early enough to send mail? She'd just arrived last night.

Wrapped in her towel, she sat on the bed and slid her finger under the flap to open the mysterious letter. And that's when things got weird.

## Chapter Ten

Zach knocked on Max's door thirty minutes after he'd watched her disappear upstairs. He'd had plenty of time to shower and dress. He knew women usually ran late, but something about her saying ten minutes and then not showing bothered him.

"Hey, I thought you were a 'ten-minute woman,'" he said through the oak panel. When he knocked again the door swung open. "Now a man would never say anything like that, even about a showe—"

He stopped teasing when he saw her face. She was slumped on the bed encased in another towel, clutching an envelope and a sheet of paper with a shell-shocked look in her eyes.

He sat beside her on the mattress. Her skin was cold and damp. "Max, what's wrong?" He gently took the paper out of her hand without asking. It was a single page, type-written in large font.

Dr. O'Neil,
Why do you refuse to let the town of Reddington live? The caverns belong to all of us. For this crime you will DIE, BITCH, DIE!

There was a red smear across the bottom of the page. Very dramatic and extremely creepy. All in all it appeared to be from a real whack job. One that had obviously scared the hell out of Max.

"Max, look at me. Are you okay?" He put a hand on her bare shoulder. She looked up at him with a glassy, glazed expression.

He repeated the question.

"Yes, I'm fine. I…" She shook her head as if trying to clear it. "I think so. That was…surprising. Who would…who would send this?"

"I don't know. A real head case that's for sure. Let me see the envelope."

She started to hand it to him but he stopped her, pulling a tissue from her bedside table before he took the envelope from her. "I doubt the police can help much, but there's no reason to get my fingerprints on it, too."

She nodded and handed it over. "No return address, of course."

He looked at the plain business stationery. "It's dated day before yesterday. So they knew you were coming before you got here. That doesn't make sense." The scent of her freshly washed hair and skin enveloped him as he sat beside her on the bed. She used some kind of citrus shampoo or soap. He wanted to touch her, mark her again as his.

And where had that come from? He was supposed to be focused on taking care of her, not having sex with her. Acutely aware that she was covered in next to nothing, he stood to get away from temptation. But he couldn't keep his eyes off all that exposed creamy skin. He remembered exactly how it had felt. How it had tasted.

"Who would know? Who would care?" she asked, pulling his thoughts back to the present problem.

"How about that whole roomful of folks downstairs?"

"You really think someone on the team could have sent this?" she asked.

Zach shrugged. "They're the ones who knew you were coming day before yesterday."

She met his gaze for a full minute before becoming extraordinarily uncomfortable. Initially, he didn't pick up on it. He was trying so hard to appear unaffected himself by her naked nearness. Then the light dawned. She was worried about what other folks thought of him in her room right now.

Well, he didn't give a rat's ass about that. This note changed all the ground rules they'd discussed earlier. If she was being threatened, he was sticking around and he didn't care what people thought, including Max.

His job was to protect the people on the team. Although if he were honest with himself, guarding her was no real hardship. He'd originally thought he'd have to worry about them only in the cavern, but that appeared to be changing.

He hadn't been hired as a full-time bodyguard, but now with Max's situation he was taking on that role. He didn't want to stop and examine what that meant or where it was coming from. He just knew that from now on he wasn't leaving her alone.

"Max, get dressed and we'll try and figure this out while we get something to eat. This can be sorted out."

The uncertainty on her face tugged at him, but there was nothing else to be done right now. She was dead on her feet. She needed to eat and go to bed or she'd be wiped out for what was shaping up to be a very full day tomorrow.

Max didn't move.

"Come on, get dressed and I'll take you down to dinner."

That seemed to stir her up. Actually it seemed to piss her off. Anything was better than the glassy-eyed ghost who'd been sitting here moments before. "I don't need to be taken to supper like a child," she pouted.

He nodded with satisfaction, but didn't smile. She'd had a crappy day. "Okay, then you can take me to dinner. I don't like to eat alone. Just get some clothes on or I'm taking you to bed. You can't sit around in front of me half-naked and expect me to do nothing about it."

That got her moving. She glanced at him and what he saw in her eyes had him taking a deep breath. He shouldn't make suggestive comments he had no intention of following through on.

She hopped up like a jackrabbit and flew into the bathroom, slamming the door behind her. But not before he caught a glimpse of her sweet ass behind that pitiful towel she had wrapped around her breasts. Unfortunately for Zach, the terry cloth was more substantial than the tiny threadbare version she'd worn last night.

He would have made another "motivating" remark, but he'd seen the hefty bottles and jars she had in her toiletries kit. He wasn't taking a chance she'd throw something at his head. Something told him she had very good aim.

Zach stepped out of Max's room and walked to his own, dialing his cell phone. Kirk answered on the second ring.

"It's Zach. We've got a problem."

"Explain."

Ten minutes later, Kirk knew that Zach knew exactly what kind of research was going on in Devil's Hollow. And Zach had permission to extend the night watchman's hours to 24/7 for the cave. Earlier in the day a guard had been hired for the evenings, but the letter put a whole new twist on things.

Zach now had orders from Kirk not to leave Max alone. There was no way his boss could know that Zach had no intention of leaving Max by herself, but it was nice to have that as part of his job description. She wasn't going to like the last set of orders or how Kirk proposed they stage them.

In fact, Max was going to hate it.

Zach hoped his peace offering would smooth the way. He'd learned a little bit from his twin sister over the years. He smiled ruefully as he knocked on Max's door with a tray of food.

She answered, this time in a robe, fuzzy socks and with a stormy expression. "You called Kirk."

"Yes, as you've reminded me before, he's my boss."

"You told him what happened." She blocked the doorway.

"That's right."

"Complete with my freak-out in the cave?"

"No, I told you I wouldn't tell anyone about that."

She sighed and shook her head. "Damn, I knew I gave that away myself."

He cocked an eyebrow. "You gonna let me in?"

She eyed the two plates and the wine bottle on the tray. "Who knows you're up here with that?"

"Mrs. Mabry…and probably Sal. I told her you were wiped out and had to make some phone calls. I passed Sal on the way up the steps."

"And he's rooming with Rodger." She scowled and crossed her arms. "We talked about this."

"Before you got that letter."

"I told you I didn't want people to know."

Zach shrugged. "Mabry'd already figured it out. Besides, the letter makes it a moot point."

She stared at him a moment longer, trying to look tough.

"Food's gettin' cold," he said.

She gazed at the tray and her eyes went soft and dreamy. He'd like to make her look that way without a tray of food in his hands.

"What do you have there?" She reached over and answered her own question by lifting the napkin. "Oh my God, biscuits and meatloaf and…brownies!" She stared at the wine. "Because that's merlot, I forgive you."

There was only one glass on the tray. Max searched his face one last time, reached for the front of his shirt to tug him into the room and he was lost. He was glad he had the food in his hands or he would have done something crazy like tumble her onto the mattress. She plucked a biscuit from the plate as he set the tray on her dresser desk.

"I could eat a horse," she mumbled around the bread in her mouth and picked up the corkscrew beside the plates. She studied it for two seconds before thrusting the bottle and opener into Zach's restless hands. "I'm awful at this."

He cracked a wry grin, surprised she would admit it and that she was over her mad so quickly. She didn't miss the look he gave her. "Yes, I know. I like to control most things, but I'm a snob about wine. I hate having cork floating in my glass and I always end up screwing up the opening."

"Just most things?"

She ignored his smart-ass comment. "So why did you call Kirk without me?"

"I wanted to tell my version of the day." He was grateful she'd given him something to do with his hands. The cork released with a small *pop*.

"And?" She took the wine from him and poured a very full glass of the merlot in the fine crystal Zach had brought up with her tray. Without asking him, she poured another generous serving into the empty water glass on her desk.

"I wanted to extend the night watchman's hours."

"Yes, he told me that."

"Anything else?" She handed Zach the water glass of wine.

"You know what else. He wants me to stick close to you."

Zach drank his merlot and watched as she closed her eyes and took a deep sip before answering him. There wasn't any place for him to sit except the bed and he wasn't doing that and staying sane, so he leaned against the bedpost.

"He mentioned it to me." She took another taste of the wine and studied him as she leaned against the wall. Her damp hair from the shower curled around her shoulders and her robe was loosely belted at the waist. "And what did you think of his plan for how that should work?"

Zach had an immediate and vivid mental picture of tugging that belt open and exploring her curves under the terry cloth. He cleared his throat before speaking. "The idea that we should pretend we're having a hot affair?"

She nodded. "What do you think?"

"I thought we'd already discussed it." He put his wine down. She continued to study his face as he took her glass and put it beside his on the desk. Before she could object, he had her against the wall with his hands inside her robe. He skimmed his palms up her back, pulling her toward him.

She gasped in his ear. The power that surged through him at the sound was palpable. "We could talk about it some more," he murmured.

"Maybe." Her eyes were cautious as he leaned in to kiss her, but she wrapped her arms around his neck.

He stopped millimeters from her lips. "Well, Max, we wouldn't have to sneak around. And you know for a fact that we're compatible in this area. We'd certainly be able to pass the time."

"Yes, there is that," she breathed. Her hands were twined in his hair as he looked into her eyes. She leaned forward to close the gap and again, he was lost.

"So you think we can work with this?" he asked, coming up for air.

He heard the smile in her voice. "Yes, yes, I do." She slid a hand down to untuck his shirt as she spoke. Her mouth was on his neck.

His hands were busy unknotting the belt at her waist and his lips were on hers when a knock at the door had them jumping apart like guilty teenagers. They took a shaky breath in unison and stared at each other. "I suppose this should be funny," he said, running an unsteady hand through his hair.

"How come we're not laughing?" Her eyes were no longer filled with the teasing light from moments before. She pulled her robe together and tried to smooth her hair. "Who is it?" she called.

"It's Sal. I got preliminary reports on the specimens we collected."

She met Zach's gaze, her face stark, begging him without words.

"Come on, Max," he whispered. "It's a helluva lot easier this way."

"Just a minute, Sal."

Zach shook his head, trying to ward off what he knew was coming.

"Can't you wait in the bathroom until he leaves?" she pleaded.

He slipped his hand back into her robe and slid it past her waist to her hip. "You are kidding, right?" he asked.

"No, I'm not."

He tightened his grip on her hip, ever so slightly. "I'm not going anywhere. Get used to it till this is over."

## Chapter Eleven

Max stared at a point over Zach's shoulder, and something in her face changed before she met his gaze again. She nodded. "You're right. Go get the door. Just please, don't swagger."

He tried to look offended. "I never swagger."

"Right." She rolled her eyes. "I'm getting dressed." She stalked to the bathroom for the second time that night and slammed the door. Outside, thunder rumbled and the windows shook.

Zach was glad she wasn't there to see him grin. He tucked in his shirt and opened the door to Sal, who looked puzzled for all of three seconds. The man was the equivalent of a rocket scientist, after all. Sal took in the dinner plates, the glasses of wine and got up to speed real quick. "Ah, okay. So you're, um... I didn't realize you two—" Sal blushed.

"Max is changing. She'll be out in a minute." Zach opened the door wider.

Sal recovered and now glared.

Zach felt like he was waiting on his date for the prom to come downstairs. He could see why Max hadn't wanted this news out there with her team.

"Hey, Sal, what do you have?" Max stepped from the bathroom in jeans, a T-shirt, bare feet and her damp hair still curling around her shoulders.

Sal stared pointedly at Zach.

"It's okay, Sal. If I'm sleeping with him, we're talking in front of him. Zach knows what we're really doing here."

Sal again blushed like a schoolboy, stammered but kept going. He reached into the backpack he'd brought with him, obviously anxious to change the subject. "It's one of the bottles from the collection. Rodger was setting up a makeshift lab in our room with the equipment we salvaged. He was able to save more than we thought."

Sal dug around in the pack. "Rodger had a pocket alkalinity meter in his gear here at the Lodge. We were going to try to culture one of the specimens just to see if we could grow anything in fetal bovine serum." Sal pulled a blackened specimen jar from a paper sack. "Look what we got."

"I don't understand. This is a sample from this afternoon?" Max asked.

Sal nodded. "I took two, Tim took three, you took one. This is one of mine. It was fine at the pond. I checked all the bottles before I put them in my pack. I didn't examine them again until we got home from getting Tim settled at the hospital. I never opened any."

The specimen was dark, no longer the clear liquid Zach had seen them putting into the jars at the pond.

"Could the specimen be contaminated?" asked Zach.

"Not unless they all are." Sal pulled two more jars from his bag and set them on the bed. They were the same color. "This one is mine, this one is Max's."

Max studied the bottles. "I don't suppose it's completely out of the question given the sabotage, but that seems awfully subtle for the same folks who shattered our microscopes and poked holes in the battery packs."

"What about the environment the bacteria are used to? I mean, we just dumped them in sterile jars. Could they be so delicate that they need a protein or chemical bath to survive outside the cave's atmosphere?" asked Sal, hunting for a place to sit.

"There's no way to know till we get down there with more equipment. Right now we've got more questions than answers," said Max.

"We need to talk to Ellen Garrett. I want to know how she got the bacteria into the lab and kept them viable."

She sighed. "I hope Kirk's equipment gets here in the morning. After talking with Ellen we'll be better prepared to try again. Ideally we need to do all the tests and experiments inside the cave if we can."

Zach raised an eyebrow as the wind picked up and rain began to splatter against the window with a renewed vigor. "That's going to be a challenge. How do you think Ellen did it?" he asked.

"I don't know. We talked quite a bit in general terms about her research last night, but I didn't realize she wouldn't be going down with us today. I honestly didn't think about it at the time we made the call this morning with all the distractions of the vandalism. She wanted to help Rodger salvage the equipment, so I let her stay topside."

"Don't beat yourself up about it," said Sal. "Salvaging that equipment was pretty damned important, too."

"Thanks, but she and I are going to have a very in-depth conversation right away. Do you know where she is now?"

Zach spoke up. "She went home. Tim's accident shook her up. She'll be back in the morning." He looked at them, decided now was the time. They had to know. "Look, I don't know how many more trips we're going to be able to make into Devil's Hollow before the pool floods."

"What?" Max's voice went up an octave.

"When Michael and I left you gathering samples and went down to check the corridor below, the water was rising fast. With this rain, there's no way to know how soon the flooding will reach the pond."

"So besides not knowing if we can even get these bacteria to reproduce, we could be running out of time?" asked Sal.

Zach nodded.

"Then it's all the more important I talk to Ellen right away. Do you have her number?" Max rummaged for a piece of paper and a pen.

Zach looked at her, really studied her a moment. She wouldn't meet his gaze, but he took in the shadows under her eyes, the exhaustion lining her face. He hadn't noticed it earlier. He'd been too busy kissing her.

"Give her and yourself a break, Max. There's nothing you can do till tomorrow, anyway." Zach held up a hand to ward off her protests. "We all need some rest."

Zach leaned against the wall he had Max against earlier and refused to let his mind dwell on how she'd felt pressed against him in her terry robe and nothing else. She glanced up from her bare feet to meet his gaze. He wondered if she was thinking the same thing.

"You know I'm right," he said.

"I don't have to like it," she muttered. Outside, the wind picked up and rain splattered against the window. She kept staring at him. The heat in her eyes told him she was thinking about what they'd been doing before Sal knocked on the door.

Sal gathered the specimen jars, oblivious to the sexual undercurrents in the room, or ignoring them. "I'll see you at breakfast. We'll talk to Ellen and figure out what's going on, Max. Don't worry." He picked up the last bottle. "You don't suppose it's mutated, do you?"

Like flipping a light switch, Max broke eye contact with Zach and reached for the specimen jar filled with dark-colored water.

"I don't even want to think about that," said Max under her breath.

"What? You think it's possible the bacteria may not even eat the cancer cells anymore?" asked Zach. He didn't add, if it ever did in the first place.

"Could be," said Max, stronger this time. "That's what

we're here to find out. But there's no way to know until we get this first problem figured out." She glared at Zach. "Don't borrow any more trouble than we've already got."

The quick flare of temper he saw was born of frustration and exhaustion. That was only fair. He understood the feeling.

"All right," he said. "Let it go for tonight. Tomorrow is going to be a marathon."

Sal nodded. "I agree. Let's table this discussion until we can talk to Ellen. Right now we're only guessing at what's going on in Devil's Hollow."

Max agreed. Not willingly. Zach could tell. But she knew when she was outnumbered and exhausted.

When Max closed the door behind Sal she rounded on Zach. "Was that necessary?" she demanded.

"Was what necessary?"

"All that posturing you did? I know you don't believe in this, but do you have to be an ass about it?" She scowled at him from across the room.

"What you are talking about, Max? I never said a word about what I did or didn't believe. You're the one who told Sal I was sleeping with you."

She shrugged uncomfortably. "That was what we agreed to."

"Yes, we did. So why are you so upset about it?"

"I don't know." She sighed and stomped to the bathroom. "I'm getting ready for bed." Her voice floated from the open doorway. "Okay, I do know. It's that I've always worked so hard to prove I'm one of them. I've never used sex or my looks to get ahead, when quite frankly there were times it would have made my life much easier if I had."

He heard water running in the sink and let her talk. She was so tightly wound, she needed to decompress. He could think of better ways to do it, but he was willing to go along with her method for a while. She obviously needed to feel like she was in control.

"You know, if I'd been willing to flirt or just pretend, my

career would have advanced quicker. This was all before Earth Pharm. I had managers before I worked here who made it clear that, if I slept with them, promotions would be forthcoming. I never did it, though. I refused."

She stepped out of the bathroom, once again in her robe.

"I almost got booted from my doctorate program because I slapped a professor for copping a feel. It's the one thing I never stooped to doing. And now I'm…"

"And now you're sleeping with me. Or telling everyone you are."

She closed her eyes and pinched the bridge of her nose before contemplating him. "You're right. I am very tired. And I'm ready to go to bed. You said you were staying here with me. Where are you going to sleep?"

He stopped himself from laughing out loud. She wouldn't appreciate that at all. Instead he eyed the queen-size bed and stared pointedly back at her. "I think we can both fit."

She didn't answer.

"Max, I'm not sleeping on the floor. But I certainly won't force myself on you."

She slowly walked over to stand in front of him. The belt on her robe was loose and he could see some kind of silky material underneath. He couldn't look away from her hypnotic blue eyes.

"That's just the thing. I'm afraid I want you just as much as you seem to want me. Though Lord knows why. I realize I've been a pain in the butt tonight." She slipped out of the robe and let it puddle at her feet.

"I've gotten kind of used to it, Max." He put his hand on the material at her waist and felt the silk slide against his fingertips.

She put her arms around his neck and pulled herself closer. "It's like you're some kind of drug and I've become addicted." Once again her fingers twined in his hair at the base of his neck.

He smiled at the sensation. It was like her hands belonged

there. His own arms automatically slid around her back. When had anything with Max become automatic? He ignored that thought and where it was headed as he lowered his mouth to hers.

"Don't sign up for rehab on my account. I like the way you handle addiction. This diving right in works for me."

Max laughed as they tumbled onto the mattress. She worked on untucking his shirt and the button of his jeans.

"Let me introduce you to a new kind of remedy," he murmured in her ear. His hand skimmed over her hips and he slipped one of the skinny straps from her shoulder.

"Hmm. And that would be what exactly?" She almost had the zipper down on his pants.

"Complete and utter abandonment to the moment." *As far away from being in control as possible.* He slid the other strap from her shoulder and pulled the gown from her body so she was finally, gloriously naked.

He pulled back for a minute to look at her. She was amazing. All creamy skin and rounded curves. Long legs that went for days. And the ass he hadn't been able to stop thinking about since this morning and that had practically gotten him killed on the climb into the cave. He wasn't teasing anymore. This was serious business.

"Yeah, I figured that's what you'd—" Whatever she'd been about to say was lost as Zach kept her busy with his own version of therapy.

*RAIN PELTS THE ROOF as I glance at the computer clock and sip my whiskey. Time is getting away tonight. I have places to go. People to see.*

*But I'm finding it difficult to leave the computer. The acts taking place on-screen hold no appeal for me. It's more what those acts represent. This plan is working better than originally intended.*

*Who knew a disgruntled untenured professor could provide such dividends? The committee of renegade pharmaceutical*

CEOs have certainly gotten their money's worth since they bribed Weatheridge's rival in the biochemistry department. They have all the original reports and testing on the bacteria. Between my letter delivered earlier today and the news about the specimens brought up from the cave, my position can hardly improve.

Everyone accepts me as Mrs. Mabry. The Earth Pharm team has no idea the real Mrs. Mabry died in a fiery car crash on her way to a job interview. Her car went over a ravine, never found, never even reported lost, since a "Mrs. Mabry" did indeed show up for her interview at Whispering Pines. The accident today with Tim Ryan was a bonus snafu. The argument with Carl Madden, heard by almost everyone at the Lodge, was pure serendipity.

The intensity of the relationship between Zach Douglas and Max O'Neil would be worrisome except I predicted something would happen between those two. The letter Max received combined with the events of today simply sped the process.

The committee will be thrilled with my latest report about the bacteria. No one predicted the problem with gathering the bacteria specimens. That information is invaluable.

The Earth Pharm scientists will certainly find a way around the issue, so I'll have to act quickly. But the job will be infinitely easier now, particularly after tonight. It'll require one sacrificial lamb, but I knew that going in.

There's nothing happening on-screen right now that the committee needs to hear about. Well, nothing that's going in my report, anyway.

Even so, there are three committee members who would be very interested in seeing and hearing about this part of the evening's activities. I know from previous experience and I suppose I could burn a DVD of the action, just for the hell of it. But I don't really want to. I'm not into that.

However, you never know when a tape like this could come in handy. Because neither of the subjects is married or *attached, I'm not going to bother. I'm not being paid to feed the committee's baser appetites and I do have a conscience.*

*I finish my whiskey and slip on my rain jacket. The camera will catch any activity I miss. Phase two of the committee's plan officially begins tonight.*

## Chapter Twelve

Carl Madden huddled under the overhang at the entrance to Devil's Hollow—waiting and watching it rain. The caller had promised to meet him here, but the prearranged hour was long past. Carl wasn't going to make the deadline for *The Reddington County Herald* tonight.

It still bugged the hell out of him that he hadn't recognized the voice. He knew everyone in this backwater hick county, or he'd thought he did. He hadn't even been able to tell if it was a man or a woman. He wondered if he'd been had.

He'd been ducking Zach Douglas's night watchman for the past forty-five minutes. The man had just climbed into his truck and driven off for what Carl assumed was a call of nature. No wonder. The old gentleman had guzzled a Thermos full of coffee while Carl had hunkered down behind some rocks in the open field, rain pelting down on his head about ten yards from the sheltering overhang. He probably had twenty minutes before the watchman would be back from the Gas N' Go filling station out on Highway 281.

The caller had been so specific. Diamonds in Devil's Hollow. And Carl could have the exclusive. Maybe it would be enough to lift him out of the obscurity that was the one-horse, nowhere, hole in the road he'd been wasting away in since his disgrace and dismissal from the real world. At least that's what Carl called it. A divorce and a bender is how the rest of the world viewed his situation.

He lay in the mud at the edge of the overhang and peered into the cave's unusual opening.

"Helloooo?" His voice echoed into the deep cavern, muffled by steadily falling rain. No one was going to show. He knew it in his bones. He might as well go home.

Soaked to the skin, he wished hard for a beer. He hadn't had one in three years, so he wouldn't start drinking tonight over a "no show" informant. But it was a nice fantasy.

He clamored to his feet and turned to leave the overhang for the slog back through the mud and rain to his truck. He'd parked a half mile away. In this downpour, that had been overkill. If he didn't slip and fall on his ass, he'd be lucky.

Suddenly a slim shadow blocked his path.

"Oh, there you are. I didn't think you were coming—" He stopped. "Mr.—"

He caught the flash of the knife, just before it dug into his chest.

*"Why? You?"*

He dropped his flashlight. The pain was so fast and so sharp, at first he didn't realize what had happened, then he couldn't breathe.

The light on the ground threw odd shadows, but he could still see the cool, detached eyes of his attacker—eyes that never acknowledged his question. Perhaps he hadn't spoken it aloud. With what felt like a punctured lung, he realized he couldn't speak. He'd never been quite so wrong about a person's character before.

As Carl struggled for breath, his attacker opened a small packet and dumped something over his chest and stomach. He desperately gasped for air as more blood pumped onto the rocks beneath him and mingled with the rain. He coughed and blood splattered over his chin and face.

Whatever had been scattered over his chest and midsection

fell to the ground around his body. He brought his hand up to his belly and felt the substance there.

It was…a pebble?

He wasn't strong enough to lift it, to look at it. Instead, he curled his fist around the small odd-shaped stone as his hand fell to his side.

Rain continued to fall, washing his blood over the rocky soil beneath him. His attacker watched, admiring the red patterns mingling with the raw diamonds on the ground. By morning the rain would wash most of the blood from the gemstones and rock into the soil, but it would still make for a stunning murder scene.

The sacrificial lamb. Exactly what had been ordered. Whatever it took to stop Earth Pharm's research from going forward in Devil's Hollow.

MAX LAY UNDER the covers listening to the rain. Six a.m. What was she doing here? She'd just spent the night with Zach.

Talk about out of the frying pan and into the fire. What the hell was she doing to her life? She certainly knew how to pick unsuitable men. Zach thought she was lying to herself about the viability of Earth Pharm's project. So of course she'd set out to prove him wrong by hopping into bed with him.

Hadn't her experience with Robert taught her anything?

She rolled over to face a wall of sleeping muscular back. Touching his shoulder would be a bad idea…mirroring all her other poor choices of the past twenty-four hours.

Zach lumped her into the same group of people who'd murdered his sister. She gave herself a mental shake as she quietly slid out of bed. Zach lay on his side. Covers low on his waist. Looking like temptation personified. If she lingered, she'd be snuggled up beside him forgetting all about how wrong they were for each other.

Was it just yesterday he'd told her how his sister had died?

She couldn't quite believe he blamed the entire pharmaceutical industry for that. Including Earth Pharm. Worse still, she couldn't believe she'd slept with him.

It must have been exhaustion or heat stroke, except it hadn't been that hot yesterday. She contemplated his smooth muscles and well-defined chest. It had been lust, pure and simple, and she'd better own up to it. He'd done an awesome job of making her forget her troubles and the fact that he didn't believe in what her company was trying to accomplish here.

Max wasn't one to lose control and it certainly never happened in bed. But with Zach, she'd practically forgotten her name. How did he do that exactly?

She was going to have to stay far, far away from him or she was going to be in deep trouble. She headed to the bathroom to get a shower and a grip. It was that or crawl back in bed with the devil.

ZACH HEARD THE shower running and debated whether to join Max or let her stew.

Morning-after regrets.

He'd guess Max was filled with them. Last night neither of them had been willing to consider all the factors involved. He sighed heavily because no one was there to hear him, then sat up and strode into the bathroom.

The exhaust fan was so loud he was able to use the toilet, wash his hands and borrow Max's mouthwash without her hearing him. The air was steamy and smelled like her citrus shampoo. Without warning he pulled the shower curtain aside and stepped inside the tiny enclosure. She gave a small squeal. Suds covered her head and bubbles sluiced down her breasts and thighs. His body was happy to see her.

"God, Zach, you scared me to dea—"

He leaned down and stopped her protests with a soul-searching kiss. Somewhere between the bedroom and gargling he'd decided he wasn't going to let her object or even think about why this was a bad idea.

And he wasn't going the think about it, either. About how she was infuriating as hell but under his skin at the same time. He had to work at the kiss, but her protests dissolved with the soap bubbles. He sought a better grip on her slippery body and pulled her to him.

"Good morning," he said, skimming a hand down her thigh. He smiled before kissing his way across her collarbone to the top of her breast. Warm water beat down on the back of his head.

"'Mornin' to you, too." She hissed in a breath as he took her nipple into his mouth. "What are you doing?" She pulled back.

He cocked an eyebrow as he slid to his knees. "Dr. O'Neil, do I need to draw you a picture?" He enjoyed watching her eyes widen as he cupped her ass and pulled her toward him again. Her skin was slick and hot.

A smiled played across her lips. "No, I just wanted a little narration," she murmured.

"Well, let's just say I'm melting your resistance."

*I'M DRESSING AND watching the computer screen at the same time this morning. Because I didn't get much sleep last night, I only had time for a quick shower myself at 5:00 a.m. It took a couple of hours to write the report. The committee has it now, along with my recommendations. Their answer should be arriving at any moment.*

*Phase two is already well under way. Anonymous phone calls have been made. Local fireworks will begin shortly. I can't be late. Today is pivotal.*

*The bathroom camera's lens is all fogged over. Looks like Dr. O'Neil and Douglas are going at it in the shower. Well, they'd better enjoy themselves. This is the last bit of peace those two are going to enjoy. Too bad. Looks like they got less sleep than I did.*

*Well, that only makes my job easier.*

*The e-mail arrives and I read it with a sense of satisfaction and a surprising tickle of dread. The committee has taken my recommendations a step further than the original proposal. What is being suggested will definitely solve the committee's problem, but will it devastate the area beyond the point of recovery?*

*This has never come up before. Then again, the stakes have never been quite so high, nor the consequences so dire.*

*It all comes down to conscience versus reputation.*

*That could be amusing. But I'm not laughing.*

MAX TURNED OFF the hairdryer and set it on the tile countertop. Zach's voice carried through the closed door. He was talking to someone in *their* room.

Should it bother her that she was starting to think of it as *their* room? She didn't let herself dwell on that disturbing thought.

She wore a floor-length robe, but she wasn't walking out there not knowing who was in the room. Max wasn't a prude, but she also wasn't going to flaunt her one-night stand, or fling, or whatever this thing with Zach was turning into. She adjusted the faucet to mask her delaying tactic.

Feeling like a cross between a five-year-old and James Bond, she bent down and peeked through the antique keyhole. The bedroom was filled with people. She was thankful for the robe this time, instead of the washcloth-size towel of two nights before.

Michael was there along Zach and two men Max didn't recognize. Zach glanced at the bathroom door a moment, and kept talking. "I left the cavern around six with Dr. O'Neil. Fred here came on at seven. That was the agreement."

The older man was nodding his head. Max assumed this Fred was the night watchman. "That's right. I went for a comfort break at twelve-fifteen. I was gone maybe fifteen minutes. Just time enough to take a leak and get some more coffee. Rest of the night, I stayed in my truck. It was a toad strangler out there." Thunder punctuated his words. Rain was pouring again this morning.

Zach turned to the younger of the two men. He was big and bulky. Almost as tall as Zach but heftier. "What time did you find the body?"

*Body? Whose body?*

"This morning, right after it got light," said the younger man. "We don't know how long he'd been there. His clothes were saturated from the rain and the blood was washed away."

"Well, we know it was sometime after ten because Carl Madden left here around ten last night."

*Jesus.* That reporter was...dead?

The big man's head came up and he pulled a Lilliputian-size notebook from his pocket. "Really? What time was he here abouts? He told his editor he was meeting someone on a story. Asked them to hold his deadline."

Max tasted bile in the back of her throat, but didn't leave her keyhole. She saw a badge on the large man's chest and took a closer look at his clothes. The belt, the shirt. He was wearing a gun. A sheriff of some sort. He was still talking.

"When Madden didn't report, the paper was pissed. Had to fill his space with something last-minute. They didn't suspect he'd been murdered. He's a recovering alcoholic, so the editor thought he'd had a relapse. It'd be helpful to know what Madden was working on."

Suddenly Max'd had enough of skulking behind doors. She straightened and stepped into the room. "Carl Madden was here to talk to me about Earth Pharm's research."

The sheriff started, then seemed to absorb the fact that she was barefoot and wearing a robe, and that Zach was wearing only jeans. For the first time, he seemed to really look around the room and put two and two together.

An opened wine bottle was beside the bed, along with two glasses. Even Max was surprised to see Zach's open suitcase on the desk beside her bra and silky bikini panties. He must have gotten his luggage after their shower.

Zach spoke first. "Max, this is Sheriff Harris and Fred Wilkins. Gentlemen, this is Dr. O'Neil."

The older man tilted his head. "Good morning."

The bear-size sheriff nodded. "Doctor, what did Mr. Madden have to say exactly?"

She never broke eye contact. "That Tillman was filing for bankruptcy and the good citizens of Reddington deserved to see exactly what was going on in Devil's Hollow, right away. I explained that it was impossible due to the nature of the research. He mentioned some craziness about diamonds. I don't have a clue where that is coming from. Madden didn't want to hear me."

"Carl Madden was murdered last night at Devil's Hollow," said Zach.

She nodded. "I heard you." She couldn't manage to suppress the shudder. "I can't quite believe it. That note seems a lot more threatening now."

"What note?" asked Harris.

She handed over the envelope and letter she'd received last night.

"Was he angry when he left?" asked Harris. He held the paper by a tissue as he read it before shoving the missive into a plastic bag with a zippered top.

"We both were. I called him an idiot." Max saw no reason to hedge on the truth, even though she felt bad about the incident now. Several people had overheard that conversation. The sheriff might as well hear about it from her. She wasn't going to give him reason to suspect her of anything other than impetuous judgment where her sleeping arrangements were concerned.

"But I didn't kill him. I was right here all night long. And yes, I have an alibi." She stared pointedly at Zach, then back at the sheriff. Who knew a one-night stand could be so empowering?

Fred blushed like a virgin. The sheriff went beet red all over his bald head but nodded. "Gotcha. Well, if you think of anything that might help us, please give me a call."

She started to let it go, then spoke up. "There was one thing."

"Yes?" The sheriff turned back to face her.

"Carl said he was talking to our competitors. Implying Earth Pharm's. I have no idea which one or who it could be. Is that significant?"

Harris jotted down more notes in his tiny book. "I'm not sure, but we'll check it out." The man was now looking for a fast way out of the room and Michael offered it.

"Let me walk you both down," he said. "Mrs. Mabry may have some muffins ready now. Y'all can take some for the road if you like."

Fred and Sheriff Harris followed him out, closing the door behind themselves.

Max leaned against the desk. "This is horrible. That reporter, Carl. Dead."

"Yes, it's hideous." Zach wasn't looking at her very sympathetically. In fact, he looked furious. "What the hell is going on, Max? What did you *not* tell me yesterday about the research at Devil's Hollow?"

Max couldn't meet his eyes. She'd dreaded this conversation so much. "You do realize there are other people after this research, right? I mean, we're not the only people looking for a cure for cancer."

"Of course."

"Some of them don't necessarily want a cure to be found."

"I don't— What do you mean exactly?" he asked.

She heard the sharpness in his tone and fought the urge to focus on her feet instead of meeting his eyes.

"I know this will sound paranoid. Scientists in medical research are an incredibly paranoid bunch. We practically encrypt our grocery lists. But this is real. Think about all the money that is made in cancer treatment, Zach. Besides just the people who would like to be first with the cure, there are people who would rather no cure was ever found."

"Why?"

"It would cut into profits if there was no need for cancer treatment."

Zach nodded. "So all that business about being first and not having any idea about who was threatening you was a lie?"

"No, that's true. We had no idea that anyone else even knew these bacteria existed outside of Reddington. It's of vital importance that no one know—"

"So you were lying again," interrupted Zach, his voice glacial. "I wasn't that far off the mark after all, was I?"

"I don't consider these bottom feeders to be part of the pharmaceutical industry. They're parasites."

"That's a bit of the pot calling the kettle black, Max. Welcome to the world of capitalism. That's how it works and you better get out the way of the big machine or it will grind your bones to dust."

"God, when did you become such a cynic?"

The look of pain that shot across his face was so brief, she would have thought she'd imagined it, until he spoke. "The day they murdered my sister. You and your Earth Pharm cronies aren't much better to my way of thinking. You're all liars."

She gaped. She couldn't help herself. There was no answer for that. She didn't speak for almost a minute. He dropped his penetrating gaze. When she did finally say something, the words that came out surprised her. "Did you call Carl Madden or contact him in any way yesterday?"

His head shot up and again he pinned her with those emerald-green eyes. "What?"

"I saw you speaking to him as he was leaving here yesterday." Her stomach roiled even as she thought of the implications. Zach's attraction to her made sense now. Had he been using her?

"What are you talking about?" he asked.

"On the way out of the room last night, he spoke to you.

What did he say? Were you planning to meet him? To tell him about our research? I have to know." She hated the accusation in her voice. But this was the way her world worked. Everyone screwed you when it came to data.

"Hell no, and I can't figure out where you get off saying that."

"He leaned down and whispered something to you."

The look on Zach's face was part disbelief and part disgust. He shook his head. "Carl was saying he was sorry to hear about Tammy. We'd met right after he moved here. It was just before she died, and I hadn't seen him since I got back."

"Oh." Waves of embarrassment rolled over her. She felt like a fool.

"Why would you accuse me of—I'm not even sure what exactly. And after you lied to me. I feel sorry for you, Max. You really don't trust anyone, do you?" He shook his head. "Do you ever let anyone in past that iron control of yours? God, I'm surprised you even let me make love to you."

"That's a horrible thing to say." *I almost let you in. I almost let myself be vulnerable.* Hot tears pricked at the backs of her eyelids. Where in hell had those come from? Never again would she trust a man. And no way would she let Zach see her cry.

Even if another man was throwing her away. So what? It had happened before. She'd survive. She gathered herself and faced him with a bravado she wasn't feeling. "I only let the people in who can handle it. You obviously can't."

His detached expression chilled her more than his earlier words had. How had they ended up here when thirty minutes ago they'd been—well, as far from this as they could be? She squared her shoulders. She couldn't let herself think about that. A man was dead. She hadn't known Madden, hadn't really even liked him, but still...

"I think you'd better leave now," she said.

He shook his head. "The letter," he muttered. "As much as

I'd like to, I can't. I'm afraid, Dr. O'Neil, that we're stuck with each other."

He gave a bitter laugh and walked past her to his suitcase. Jeans rode low on his hips and the smoothly toned muscles of his back mesmerized her for a moment as he searched through his bag. She forced herself to look away, grateful it was his back that she'd been staring at. What was wrong with her? She was hurt and mad, yet still attracted to him?

"Get dressed," growled Zach. "I need to call Harris and tell him about this latest."

"Won't he be angr—" She stopped at the cool censure in his eyes.

"Probably. You withheld information, Max. But I doubt it's the first time that's happened to the sheriff." He pulled a T-shirt over his head and turned to leave, the door shutting behind him with a solid click.

"Wait." The word died on Max's lips. She wanted to call him back, wanted to call back the past five minutes. How had it gone so far off the rails so fast? How had she ended up here?

She should have told him about the possibility of other people looking for the bacteria. But she and Kirk had never expected anything like this. She'd never expected anything like Zach. What a disaster.

He was surprised they'd made love? That they'd gotten to this point so quickly? No one could have been more surprised than Max herself. She simply didn't let others in over that wall of hers. Robert had been one of the few exceptions. And look what that had gotten her. Gut-wrenching pain. Was it worth it? Her ex-fiancé and his tart secretary had proven otherwise.

Zach had gotten past her well-honed self-defense mechanisms without her even realizing it. In record time, too. This morning's ugliness was a fresh reminder as to why she had those walls and defenses in place. They kept her safe from emotional harm, shielded from pain and vulnerability. From having to let go.

Before last week Max had prided herself on leading a well-ordered life. That was before the "goodbye boff." And this project that was making her crazy. And Zach.

He qualified as a messy relationship. A fiasco. It was all spiraling out of control way too fast. While there were many things in her life over which she had no power, who she slept with was something she could fix right away. Perhaps she could regain a modicum of her sanity in the process.

# Chapter Thirteen

Zach sat at the Lodge's dining table and tried not to sulk. How in hell had it become such a mess? He hadn't even had a personal life twenty-four hours ago. He poured the cereal left out on the table and sloshed some milk into the bowl.

Where were the damn croissants they'd had yesterday?

Okay, so he was sulking.

Sal and Rodger weren't downstairs yet. That was probably a good thing. Zach was relieved to have the room to himself for a while. He wasn't fit company for anyone.

He was studying the wilting raisin bran when his cell phone interrupted his pout. He let it go to voice mail when it saw it was Harris again. His mood was so foul, he didn't want to make an enemy of the sheriff. He'd call the man back in a few minutes and tell him this latest after he had his head together.

Besides, there was nothing Harris could tell him that was going to improve his mood except that the medical examiner had made a mistake. Carl Madden wasn't really dead. He'd simply been taking a nap with a knife sticking out of his chest in front of Devil's Hollow. Hmm. Not likely.

The phone rang again. Harris wasn't giving up. Zach took a bracing sip of coffee and wished it was something stronger before he answered the call.

"Zach, it's Harris. I've got some interesting news from the M.E."

"Carl Madden's alive."

"What? What are you talking about?"

Zach shook his head even though Harris couldn't see. "Nothing, just wishing this would all go away."

"Well, sorry, I can't help you there. And Carl is deader than Hamen's housecat. But what he was holding in his hand and what was sprinkled on his body… Now, that's interesting."

"So what is it?"

"Well, I was wondering if you could tell me. What are your scientists looking for exactly in Devil's Hollow?"

Zach saw no reason to keep the research secret any longer. Madden had already died for it. "Bacteria," he said.

"Bacteria?"

"Yes, you know—the microscopic organisms. It's for cancer drug research."

"Not women's mineral makeup."

"No."

"You're sure that's all they're looking for?"

And wasn't that the $64,000 question? "To the best of my knowledge," said Zach.

"To the best of your knowledge would there be any reason for Carl Madden to have raw diamonds scattered over his body?"

Zach leaned back in his seat, the soggy cereal completely forgotten. "No, no reason whatsoever. There's no evidence of diamonds or any kind of jewel vein in Devil's Hollow that I've seen."

"Well, you're going to have a hard time convincing the townspeople of that."

"What's going on, Harris?"

"Someone made a phone call to the local radio station saying there are diamonds at Devil's Hollow and that's why Earth Pharm is being so secretive."

"Crap. Where is that coming from?"

"Rumors run rampant in small towns, Zach. You know that. But hang on to your shorts. It gets even better."

"How exactly?"

"The Internet is ubiquitous," said Harris. Zach didn't think Harris knew words that big. But he had the sense not to mention it.

"The call got picked up on a streaming station. Now the story is plastered literally all over the world. You'd better warn your people. You've got a regular shitstorm of publicity and ridiculousness coming your way. I've got some deputies out here trying to lock down the crime scene now, but I think it's fair to say that we're about to become Grand Central for crazy treasure hunters. Any idea who would do something like this?"

"Yeah. I just talked to Max some more and apparently there are folks who would like nothing more than to shut down the Earth Pharm research."

"What?"

Zach explained the situation as Max had told him.

"So did she give you any ideas as to who would do something like this?"

"No, no real leads. Just that other entities might be trying to stop this research."

"Well, it's looking like they did just that. I can't let you go back down into Devil's Hollow right now. There are already helicopters flying over the cavern with cameras. We've got twenty-five people from town out there right now and it's only nine. What do you think this will look like this afternoon or, hell, tomorrow?"

Zach remembered Sal and Max's conversation from the night before. This would be the end of Earth Pharm's project. And while he didn't necessarily believe in the project, he very much wanted back into Devil's Hollow himself.

"Harris, they want to get back down there one more time. The scientists need samples from a pool that's going to flood in a couple of days from all this rain." He paused a minute, unsure exactly why he was pushing. If Earth Pharm's access to Devil's Hollow was closed, his access would be, as well. But only until the water receded. "It's very important, vitally so."

"I don't know, Zach, this is a PR nightmare." Harris was up for reelection in just a few months.

Zach thought about the rising water and the time it would take for this mess to be straightened out. The pond would be flooded and Max's window of opportunity for research would be lost. Zach might not believe in the project and he sure as hell didn't believe in Earth Pharm. But he knew what it was like to have a dream snatched away. Telling himself he only wanted back in to map that cavern, he pushed harder.

"Harris, this goes beyond politics. The research they're doing is cancer research. It's for a cure. And those scientists have this small window of opportunity. Let them go down one last time to get the samples, that's all they need."

"I don't know."

"Think about it, Harris. A cure for cancer. You could be the one who helps them get it. Think how that would play into your bid for reelection."

Why was he doing this? He didn't want to examine his own motives too closely. Since he didn't believe in Earth Pharm, it must be for Max. Probably because his mind was still scrambled by the mind-blowing sex. Of course, that didn't seem right, either. He should be furious since she'd lied to him again about the project.

Harris's voice jerked him back to the conversation. "Jeez, Zach. That's a lot of pressure."

"Yeah, well. You're a tough guy. You can take it. I'll call you later and we can work out the details, maybe going in at night if that's easier. News choppers can't see us as well then."

"Can you do that at night?"

"Caves are all dark once you get inside, Harris. We'll go in however you'll allow us."

The sheriff hesitated and even over the phone, that pause told Zach everything. "It will have to be tonight. But no one can know or this will blow up in my face. You hear?"

"Right." Zach nodded into the phone. "I'll have them at the entrance at ten."

Zach hung up and leaned back in his seat nonchalantly. Inside, he was doing the mambo. He smelled something wonderful and realized Mrs. Mabry was at the sideboard with a basket of homemade breads.

"Good morning, Mr. Douglas. Are you getting enough breakfast?"

Zach nodded. "Yes, ma'am. Are those muffins?"

"Yes, sir." She brought over the basket and poured him a cup of coffee.

"Do you have any of those croissants like yesterday?" he asked. "They're awesome."

Mrs. Mabry smiled. "I might be able to scare some up." Sal and Max came into the dining room as Mrs. Mabry disappeared into the kitchen.

Max hesitated when she saw Zach, but he waved them over to his table. Regardless of how Max felt about him, he needed to tell them both this latest news from Harris.

Zach watched her cross the dining room. God, he had it bad. His anger had evaporated sometime during his conversation with Harris and he didn't even have to close his eyes to remember what Max looked like less than an hour ago in the shower. Her hair slicked back, steam all around them, her body pressed to his, her voice in his ear.

The look in her eyes was different now. She was shooting tiny poison darts at him. Still, the day was looking up in a weird way. Despite the whole disaster scenario at Devil's Hollow, Zach felt oddly cheerful for the first time since Harris's news. His job was going to hell, but he was about to have croissants with Max.

"DIAMONDS?" Max protested. "Where is this coming from?" She was sitting with Zach at breakfast but she didn't want to be. Sal had left to go and tell Rodger the latest and to call Ellen. Could things be any more wretched? The general public was on a wild diamond chase and the sheriff was threatening to close the cave to everyone, including Earth Pharm.

Panic and frustration washed over her. "No, we have to get down there. Just once more."

Everything was slipping out of her control. It frightened her. And Zach didn't care. That all boiled over now that they were alone.

"You don't even believe in this. You never have. You think I work for murderers. Why should I trust you?"

He raised an eyebrow and put his hand on her arm. "Trust? Who lied to whom here?" It was the first time he'd touched her since they'd made love in the shower. "We can make this happen, Max. But you've got to start trusting me."

The contact startled her. The warmth of his hand was more welcome than she realized. "Wh-what? How?"

"Let go." His expression and his tone were softer than they were earlier. "I'll make this work, Max. Don't worry. You'll get what you want." His bitterness and anger appeared to be gone, compartmentalized somewhere she couldn't see. It wasn't an about-face, because he hadn't been angry when she'd walked into the room. But she'd been furious. She wasn't sure what to do with her emotions.

She had to swallow before she answered. Everything was changing and moving so fast. She had to search for a way to find her equilibrium.

"We won't be able to go down unless the equipment arrives," she said. "We have to have the new specimen bottles and battery packs."

He smiled, but it wasn't the *GQ* grin that took her breath away. It was the wintry smile she'd gotten the first day they'd met. "Okay, I understand you still have to control it all. I guess it really is too much to hope that you could trust someone else."

"I can't," she whispered. "I'm sorry." This project was her responsibility. She couldn't let go, couldn't trust someone else with it. She'd been burned before and this was too important.

He took a deep breath and continued as if she'd never spoken. "We have battery packs out here in the sticks. And we can use carbide helmets if we have to. What we don't have are your fancy specimen jars and microscopes. I'm not sure if you'll be able to do everything you want to do in terms of your research. I think Harris will let us go down tonight after some of the crowds die down."

"Tonight?" Her voice rose and she worked to lower it. "Oh, that's wonderful. You and Michael will be with us, though, right? I'm concerned with all this rain that we could run into flooding issues."

The rich scent of buttery croissants assaulted her as Mrs. Mabry placed the basket on the table.

"Thank you, ma'am. These are incredible," said Zach.

The woman nodded, refilling his coffee cup before going back to the kitchen. "You should try one of these." Zach bit into the flaky concoction. "They're remarkable."

"No, thanks." She glanced down at his hands for a moment and remembered where they'd been on her body. She couldn't quite believe she'd—

"We'll both be there," he said, breaking into her thoughts. "Flooding is a legitimate concern, but with the delay I think you have time for the equipment to arrive."

She swallowed hard. "Great. That's really, really great." The words sounded weak to her own ears. They were being so achingly polite. He might have been the bellboy and not the man who'd made love to her in the shower an hour ago. Oh God, what had she done? Had she screwed this up beyond all redemption?

Sal arrived then with Rodger in tow. They sat and Zach ran through everything they'd just discussed.

"We need to talk to Ellen," finished Max. "We've got to figure out how she prepared those specimens."

"I just tried to call her. She must be in the shower," said Sal.

*The shower.* Max almost choked on her orange juice.

"Or in class," added Rodger. "I can't remember if she had one today or not."

Zach quickly drained his cup of coffee and stood. "You have lots of details to work out with your team. I'll check in with you later." He headed toward the door.

"Thank you," said Max.

He turned and lasered his emerald-green eyes on her. "My pleasure," he murmured. The look burned and her heart stuttered. That wasn't a bellboy look, at least not at any of the hotels where she'd ever stayed.

ZACH STOOD TEN YARDS back and watched a deputy wrestle another barricade into the dirt road in front of Devil's Hollow. The area surrounding the caverns appeared to be a regular three-ring circus and news of the diamonds was all over town.

While about thirty people were digging up clods of dirt, other would-be treasure hunters were there to get a glimpse of the crime scene and what was quickly becoming known as "the treasure cove." News crews, cameras, even a helicopter buzzed overhead as if this was a major happening. He was looking at the cumulative power of the Internet and small-town gossip. It was frightening.

The modest force of deputies for Reddington County was likely to be overwhelmed if reinforcements didn't arrive soon or the weather didn't go south again. As Murphy's Law would have it, the sun was peeking through clouds for the second time in ten days. With any luck the thunderheads in the distance would arrive in a couple of hours.

Sheriff Harris spied him from the barricades and walked over. "What do you make of this?" he asked.

"It's like nothing I've ever seen," replied Zach.

Cars pulled up every few minutes, and occasionally people hopped out into the field and began to dig.

Harris spoke up after a moment. "I have a poster in my office that says 'Never underestimate the power of stupid people in large groups.' I believe this is what they were talking about."

Another pickup truck wound its way through the labyrinth of parked cars to the barricades that blocked the road beside Harris and Zach. The driver parked in front of the flashing blockade.

They could hear the passenger's voice before the engine shut off. "What the bloody hell do you mean, you won't unload the boxes here?" The Scottish brogue was heavy as he reamed the driver. "Just because these poor souls are delusional, doesn't mean I am. We had a deal, a very rich deal. I need to have these boxes delivered as close to the entrance as possible and unloaded, then you can come back to this field and dig to China for all I care."

"Uh-oh." Zach had heard that voice before. It was Kirk and he was none too happy with the situation.

"Do you know that guy?" asked Harris, all his law enforcement instincts immediately on point.

"Yeah, I'm pretty sure he's Dr. Ralph Kirk, the man who hired me. The owner of Earth Pharm."

"Is that a situation about to get out of hand?"

"Only if that driver is dumb enough *not* to unload those boxes," said Zach.

"Do I need to step in?"

"I think Kirk can handle it," said Zach. "That's the replacement equipment."

Harris started for the truck. "All the same, I think I'd like to meet your boss."

Zach started after him. "Yes, I suppose I would, too."

# Chapter Fourteen

Zach watched the tailgate fall with a boom. The driver was hostile and if eyes were daggers, Kirk would be dead. But the CEO and owner of Earth Pharm appeared to be oblivious to the man's displeasure.

Harris introduced himself to the Scotsman.

"I hear you're up for reelection," said Kirk.

"Yes, sir. If the citizens of Reddington see fit to reelect me." One of his deputies called him over and the sheriff stepped away.

Zach reached out to shake the older man's hand, relieved yet wary to finally be meeting Max's infamous Ralph Kirk.

"So you're Zach Douglas." Kirk's grip was firm and he looked Zach over to a degree that made him distinctly uncomfortable, as if he were the pig being sized up for the company barbecue.

"It's good to meet you face-to-face, sir. This is a surprise."

Kirk continued to study him as he answered. "After the accident yesterday and all the business with the councilmen and then that letter, I felt Max needed a bit of hands-on support." Kirk paused a moment. "I believe you're taking care of some of that for us."

*Okay.* Zach wasn't sure whether that was meant figuratively or literally. "Well, I'm very glad to see you, sir. I believe Max will be also."

"Are you now?" Kirk never broke eye contact. "I'm not so sure I would be glad to see me if I were in your shoes, but I'm glad to know she's in capable hands."

No mistake. The man was speaking literally, but how was Zach to answer that? Ignoring the double entendres seemed to be the wisest course of action.

Harris came back from instructing his deputies, saving Zach from any more pointed remarks about Max. The sheriff made short work of having the boxes unloaded there at the barricades but was hesitant to move the equipment to the actual cavern entrance. Kirk asked to speak with Harris alone.

It was an odd moment, but Zach made himself scarce and went back to watching the field. There were probably fifty people actively excavating now. Moments later, Kirk waved him over.

"Sheriff Harris and I have decided that the equipment will be safe at the cavern entrance because it's so well guarded by the police."

Zach suspected this decision was the direct result of a campaign contribution for Harris's upcoming election. Mentally he seethed, but outwardly he didn't let it show. Earth Pharm was living up to his expectations. No different from Pharma-Vax. Money and campaign contributions could smooth the way for everything.

Zach and Kirk sat in silence with the equipment while Harris went to slice through the red tape involved in having the boxes secured at the actual site of the investigation. Zach had no idea what to say to his boss. He wasn't sure what to make of the outright bribery that had obviously taken place.

"Have these people gone completely insane?" Kirk wondered aloud.

"Pretty much," said Zach. "This is the shortcut to the lottery, only there's no winning ticket."

"It's a lie."

"Yes, but this area is having some hard economic times.

And this is the fairy tale." He paused for a second when he spied the group of teenagers who'd been the first to dig running from the far corner of the field. What kind of trouble were they into now?

"The reality," Kirk replied, "is, if they don't stop this outrageous digging they'll destroy the very thing that could save them."

"I know that and you know that." Zach pointed to the field. "They don't know that. I'm not sure they'd care even if they di—"

A rumbling, giant, whooshing sound shook the ground. The earth exploded and a fireball rocketed into the sky. People screamed. The sun was obliterated as dirt and rock shot into the air.

Kirk stood stunned and Zack dove for him, knocking him to the ground behind the boxes. The explosion's concussion was deafening. He could see Kirk's mouth moving, but Zach couldn't hear a thing.

They crouched behind the boxes to avoid flying rubble. Zach pushed the older man down to the asphalt as a large chunk of flaming sod came hurtling toward them. When the dust cleared there was a hole large enough to drive a tractor into at the far corner of the field. Luckily the hole wasn't over the cavern or any part of the structure of Devil's Hollow. The entire area could have caved in if that had been the case.

All around him was silence. He could see people's contorted faces, see their lips moving, but there was no sound. Most of the diggers had bloody scratches on their faces from flying bits of dirt and stone. Unbelievably, no one appeared to be seriously hurt.

Kirk had a gash on his forehead where he'd hit the asphalt and was bleeding like mad.

*Great.* He'd managed to knock his boss on his ass and practically send him to the ER within the first twenty minutes of meeting him. Right after the man had figured out that Zach had spent most of the night in Max's bed. No one could say Zach didn't make a great first impression.

He pulled off his T-shirt and ripped out the lower half to make a compress. Kirk pressed it to his head.

"I'm fine," Kirk said. Zach got that through lip reading. Kirk was struggling with the concussion-related deafness, too. But the silence was gradually being replaced with a cacophony of sound.

Suddenly Zach's sense of hearing was back full force. Noise hit with a vengeance, overwhelming in its intensity. Car alarms blared. People were shouting and crying; a few were screaming.

"I know you are," said Zach.

Kirk shook his head. He didn't understand.

"You're fine," Zach shouted, calibrating his tone. "Max would never forgive me if anything happened to you on my watch."

Suddenly Kirk could hear also. He rubbed a finger next to his ear and pulled the makeshift compress away to spear Zach with his eyes. "Really?" He was still shouting but gradually modulated his own volume to a conversational level. "Why do you say that?"

Zach took the compress away from him a moment and really looked at Kirk. This was a crazy conversation to be having right now, but then, this whole experience was so bizarre.

"Sir, you know the answer to that. We've been dancing around it since we introduced ourselves."

"Perhaps, but I'd like your version. Hell, this was my idea to begin with."

"Yes and respectfully, I have to say, it's Max's business and mine."

Kirk smiled grimly, the blood soaking his cheek. "But of course that answers my question."

Zach shrugged. This was not a discussion he wanted to be having anytime, especially now.

"I just need you to know," continued Kirk, seemingly oblivious to the chaos around them. "Working relationship aside, you hurt her, I'll make your life a living hell. Got it?"

"We're crystal clear."

"Good." Kirk seemed much more at ease than Zach would have expected. "Now can you get me up on my feet and get me out of here? I've had about all the fun I can stand for today."

HARRIS ARRIVED puffing like a steam engine, red faced and furious. "Y'all okay?" he asked, scrutinizing Kirk's head, obviously quite concerned about his latest campaign donor. "Nasty gash. You may need a stitch or two."

Kirk shrugged. "No major damage done."

"What the hell was that?" asked Zach, focusing over Harris's shoulder to see the small Reddington police force from the barricades fanned out over Farmer Tillman's plot of devastated land. The teenagers from earlier were spread-eagled on the ground. A couple were being handcuffed. Other officers were taking care of the fallen diggers.

Harris snorted in disgust. "Some punk teenagers with a barrel of gasoline, lighter fluid and a freakin' death wish. They thought they could blast away the dirt faster."

"The hubris of youth," said Kirk, remarkably calm in the face of this news. Of course, Harris was angry enough for everyone.

Zach fetched his first-aid box from the truck, while Harris stood with Kirk and fumed.

"Well, those boys'll have hubris in spades when I'm done with 'em." He shook his head and pulled a ringing cell phone from his pocket.

Zach took butterfly bandages and a bottle of sterile wash from his kit, but Harris didn't walk away. The two men couldn't help but overhear the sheriff's side of the conversation.

"This settles it. We're calling in some outside help for security. Reddington City and County can't handle this kind of situation.... Yes...I understand. We'll close Devil's Hollow for now. After that blast there's no telling what people will do to get in. Barricades will go up five miles out from here.

Thank you, Mr. Mayor." He hung up to face Zach as he was putting the butterfly bandage on Kirk's forehead.

"We may have to rethink our agreement."

"Harris, we had a deal," said Kirk, struggling not to turn his head, but glaring at the sheriff at the same time.

"Not now. We'll talk later." Harris headed to the field.

"What do you mean, not now?" called Kirk, his voice raised an octave.

The sheriff lifted his hand in parting and kept walking.

"Well, hell," said Kirk.

Zach shook his head. "You're gonna have to write a bigger check." He wasn't feeling very charitable.

Kirk transferred his glare to Zach. "I think we'd better take the equipment with us for now."

Zach nodded.

Kirk scowled after the sheriff. "It'll work out, though. Harris has a price. I just haven't found it yet."

"I believe you're right," said Zach, not bothering to hide the distaste in his voice.

People still wandered amid flaming rubble. Remarkably, some had started to dig again.

Zach started to heft a box to his shoulder, but stopped to watch the continuing chaos. "I don't understand it. That's not even where the diamonds or Madden's body were found in the first place."

"Yes, 'tis a bit of insanity. If you live long enough, you'll see the world is full of it," said Kirk.

"Isn't bacteria as a cancer cure a bit of insanity, as well?" Zach asked.

Kirk blinked and for a moment Zach was surprised he'd voiced the question aloud. But he no longer had anything to lose. He could say pretty much anything as he was no longer trying to impress his boss.

And Zach needed to know. Particularly because he was now witness to Kirk bribing a public official. Was Kirk even telling Max the truth? There was no reason to believe his boss would level with him. But the man was so filled with contradictions, so unpredictable, he just might.

"I believe these bacteria could change the course of cancer research forever. I think they might even hold the cure." He smiled sadly. "But perhaps I'm like the poor fools out there in the field, digging for diamonds where there are none. Looking for that lottery ticket. In a way I suppose Earth Pharm is like them. The cost of not digging is too great. Not believing has a cost, as well."

He stopped and gazed at the field before continuing. "Wouldn't you agree, Zach?"

Kirk's words rang in his ears. *The cost of not believing*.

Zach wasn't sure how to answer that. Zach's cost of not believing in this project would be Max. Did he want her?

He knew the answer whether he was willing to admit it to himself. He was going to have to dig deep to keep her. What would it cost him to get past his preconceived notions and believe?

# Chapter Fifteen

Covered in blood, Kirk and Zach made a dramatic entrance into the dining room without a word. Zach had debated calling ahead and decided there was nothing to be gained by warning them. Max looked up from the lunch table where she sat with her team and dropped her fork. Zach could see the worry in her eyes for Kirk and himself.

"Oh my God! Kirk? What are you doing here? What happened to you both?"

Sal and Rodger grabbed chairs for them. Mrs. Mabry got them iced tea and fussed over Kirk and his head wound.

"What happened?" asked Max again.

Kirk regaled them with his tale, kindly leaving out the part about Zach being the one who'd nearly sent him to the ER.

"So where do we go from here?" asked Sal.

"Harris is calling in more reinforcements," said Zach.

"Is he closing the cavern?" asked Max.

Kirk didn't hedge. "He wants to, but I'm still working on him. I believe he'll come around."

Max nodded. No one made any kind of snide comment and Zach realized that no one had a problem with Kirk opening the company checkbook to get them inside. This was part of why the man was here. To smooth the way for the team.

"If he does let us in I doubt we can count on more than

one trip down to the pond that's useful. The flooding," clarified Zach. "So we'll get only one chance at it. Can you handle that?"

"The biggest thing is we must know how to prepare the specimen bottles," said Rodger.

"We haven't been able to get in touch with Ellen," said Max.

"Where is she?" asked Zach, a frisson of unease running down his spine. "Has anyone seen her today?"

"No, we've been trying to reach her all morning. We assumed she was in class and forgot to tell us with all the craziness at the caverns," said Michael.

"Let's call her professor to make sure. With the Madden murder, I don't want to leave anything to chance."

Michael nodded and pulled out his cell phone.

Maybe she'd had teaching assistant duties at the university this morning and forgotten to tell them, but Ellen had been the most gung-ho about this project since the beginning. It was unlikely that calling them would have slipped her mind.

Michael flipped his phone shut in frustration. "No classes or teaching assistant's office hours today according to the department secretary. I'll run to town and see if she's home."

Zach followed him to the door. "Want company?" he asked.

Michael's eyes were awash in worry. "I do. I've got a bad feeling."

"Me, too," muttered Zach. "Let me grab another T-shirt. I'll meet you at the car."

MAX WATCHED the two men in the foyer. She wasn't letting them go see Ellen without her. She quietly slid out of her chair when Zach went upstairs. She raced to Michael's truck through the pouring rain and was waiting in the front seat when he and Zach dashed down the front steps of the Lodge. Zach did a double take when he saw her.

"What do you think you're doing?" He was climbing in and paused, body half-exposed to the rain.

"You know I have to talk with Ellen. Even if, especially if, she's ill." He was about to protest, so she steamrolled over him. "You said yourself that this is our one shot at going down into the caverns again. We have to know what she knows about prepping those specimen bottles and gathering the bacteria."

He glared at her and might have hesitated a bit longer, but it was pouring rain. With a heavy sigh, he climbed into the truck beside her.

Max couldn't help but remember the last time she'd been in a pickup with Zach. She scooted over toward the driver's side, but Michael hopped inside so that she was sandwiched in between the two large men. It wasn't exactly a hardship but the memories came rushing back when her body was pressed into Zach's.

She focused on breathing, but all she could smell was him. She was drowning in Zach. Oblivious to the riot her senses were having, Michael turned on the radio to Lady Antebellum singing about complicated situations and one-night stands. Her spine stiffened as the windshield wipers beat out the steady rhythm of the country ballad.

She finally risked a peek at Zach. His eyes were focused on the road ahead and the rapidly passing landscape. The last time she'd been in his truck appeared to be the furthest thing from his mind.

Michael hit a pothole and she was thrown toward Zach's chest. With a bench seat, there was no safe place to put her hands. Zach caught her before she ended up in his lap.

"You okay?" he asked, seemingly unaffected. She nodded and looked down at the floorboard as they untangled. Her stomach tied itself in knots. This ride-along had not been one of her better ideas.

Too uncomfortable to meet his gaze, she kept her eyes trained on the rubber floor mats. She leaned back and let her eyelids fall. Far safer to pretend to be sleepy than to risk being caught in that mesmerizing green thrall of his. She recognized her weakness and it frightened her. Once locked in, she worried she wouldn't be able to escape.

ZACH HAD BEEN to Ellen's duplex in Reddington before. He and Michael had gone after digs when first looking for Devil's Hollow. She'd even had a party once for the caving crew.

He focused on that and not the woman pressed against him as they pulled up to the apartment. Max was going to drive him nuts before this job was over.

It was a good thing Michael was with them. Zach might be doing something foolish if it were just him and Max alone. All he could think of with her practically on top of him and filling his senses was the last time they'd been in this pickup together. Zach would enjoy a repeat of that experience, but it looked like Max would rather sleep than speak to him.

A nap with Max.

Zach refused to let his mind go there. Instead, he dragged his attention back to the duplex. A student's home. Nondescript, modest.

The three dashed through the rain and huddled under Ellen's porch to knock on the front door. No one answered. Zach walked around to the back. An open sliding-glass door. Curtains billowing in the wind. A sense of dread and déjà vu unfurled simultaneously inside his chest.

Zach had read the police reports of his sister's murder. Tammy'd also had a sliding-glass door. When the police found her body, the slider was open with the curtains fluttering in an early spring breeze.

The detective on her case had finally given in and let him have the unsanitized version of the report. Zach had insisted on seeing crime-scene photos. He'd desperately needed to have the closure—to know what had happened to his twin.

Zach had badgered the man until the detective finally shoved the file at him in concerned frustration saying, "This will not help you sleep."

But the detective had been wrong. After viewing the folder's grisly contents for several hours, Zach had finally been able to rest. An added bonus, he no longer wondered if his dreams were in black and white.

His nightmares were digital HD and Technicolor. Not a bit of dreamlike fuzziness to them.

But seeing those reports had been worth it. If he had to choose between the closure that the report and photos brought and the nightmares, he'd choose to have the closure every time.

He stopped so suddenly Max ran into the back of him. He put his arm out to keep her from walking past.

"You okay?" she asked.

He shook his head.

"What's wrong?" Michael asked.

He had no idea how to answer, just that overwhelming sense of dread.

"Zach?" Max asked, pushing against his arm, trying to get under the eaves and out of the weather.

*I don't know if I can do this.*

Michael stood on the other side of him. "What's going on?"

Zach shook his head again, feeling ridiculous but cold all over at the same time.

"Does this have to do with Tammy?" Michael persisted.

Zach nodded, finding his voice. "Not sure what's wrong with me. But yeah."

"You don't have to go in," said Michael.

Zach was on the verge of agreeing before he realized that yes, he did have to go in. "No, I'll be all right."

Michael led the way and Max followed, disappearing through the filmy curtains. Zach's stomach churned at the thought of what they might find inside. He replayed Tammy's police report and transposed it over Ellen's apartment. Imagined Ellen's body in her kitchen. Her throat sliced to the back of her neck.

Before he realized what he doing, he was pushing through
the curtains, as well, the thin fabric brushing against his face.
He stood in Ellen's living room, surprised to find himself
alone. He had to get to Max and Michael. He couldn't let them
be in here by themselves.

He looked around the room and his sense of dread increased. The room was trashed. Not that Ellen was a great
housekeeper. She was a typical student from what Zach remembered from past visits, but it looked like the house had
been systematically stripped and searched. Drawers dumped
on the floor, papers strewn everywhere, even the cushions on
the sofas pulled from their rightful places and the upholstery
split. *God, no.* This was the stuff of his HD nightmares.

"Hey! Where'd you go?"

There was no answer. He started toward the back of the
house and the bedrooms.

"Michael? Max?" He tore down the hall, but his feet felt
like they were moving through molasses. "Where are you?"

# *Chapter Sixteen*

Zach found them in the master bedroom. At least that's what he assumed it was. He only caught a glimpse of Ellen, but that's all he needed to know that she was beyond their help. Blood soaked the bedspread and glazed eyes stared at the ceiling. A crime-scene photo come to life.

Michael blocked most of the view. His face ashen, he had Max by the elbow, steering her out of the room toward the hallway. "You don't want to see this, Zach," he murmured.

Shell-shocked, Zach stood in the doorway. "No." *This can't be happening. Not again.*

Max's expression was one of complete and utter horror. Finding Ellen like this was not what she had signed up for. Her face had a greenish tinge. Zach backed toward the living room on automatic pilot. The rain beat down on the roof with stunning ferocity.

"Please, I know it's hideous outside," said Max, her voice barely audible over the pouring rain, "but I can't stay in here." As if to punctuate her statement, thunder rolled and the glasses in the kitchen cabinet rattled.

"You sure?" asked Michael.

Zach looked at his friend and nodded. The entire scene had a surreal quality, like one of his nightmares, everything in stunning detail. He'd face the fury of the rain and worse to get away from it. "Let's go outside and call the police," said Zach, steering Max toward the glass slider.

Michael grabbed a large golf umbrella from a stand on the way.

The silky fabric of the curtains brushed against his face and neck, waking Zach from the dreamlike daze he'd been in. Had it been only a matter of seconds since they'd come through this door?

They stepped into the drenching rain and what felt like another world. Once outside, Zach wouldn't let Max walk away from him. She was so pale and shaky. He followed her to the edge of the patio. "Are you going to be sick?"

She shook her head. "I don't know. I'm having a hard time catching my breath."

"It's shock." He focused on Max, trying not to let himself think about Ellen being dead.

God, he couldn't. Ellen. She'd been the little sister on all the digs. They'd all looked after her and kept her safe. And now she was dead, just like Tamm—

He shut off that train of thought and sat Max down with a watery splat in one of the plastic chairs perched on the pebbled decking, completely heedless of the weather. His hand was on her back. He felt the heat of her body through her wet T-shirt and focused on it. He remembered how she'd looked the first time he saw her in the transparent blouse at the cavern. Anything, no matter how inappropriate, to get him through this without thinking about the fact that he hadn't kept Ellen safe, either.

"Take deep sips of air, Max. Slow and easy. You'll be fine. But there's no shame if you throw up, either."

She didn't look up. God, he wished she would. He needed to see her face. He needed to focus on something else besides Tammy and Ellen, dead. The rain increased, plastering their hair, their clothes to their skin.

He didn't have to think about the first time he'd met

Max. He was getting an instant replay right now. Yep, he was one sick puppy. Would serve him right if she hurled all over him.

Max finally glanced up and gave him a weak smile. Rain dripped down her cheeks and chin. "All the same I'd watch your shoes," she said.

"DON'T WORRY about that. The rain'll wash 'em off."

Max felt her smile turn to a grimace. He was being nicer than she deserved after all the nasty things she'd said to him this morning.

Lord, this was unreal. Ellen dead and that horrible scene. Even if she got rid of the pictures in her head, she'd never forget the smell.

Hanging up his cell phone, Michael joined them at the edge of the cracked decking with the golf umbrella. His face was bloodless as he put a hand on Zach's shoulder. "Harris is on the way."

They all huddled together. Michael seemed to be working on some kind of autopilot and Zach's face was unreadable.

There weren't any words to express the horror of the situation except the obvious. "I can't believe this is happening," said Max.

They lapsed into a morose silence. The rain slowed, but no one suggested getting in the truck. They were already too wet for it to matter.

Max replayed the scene in her mind over and over. It didn't matter that she was soaked to the skin, she could still smell the blood and body fluids. She studied Ellen's yard and focused on not throwing up.

Ten minutes later, Sheriff Harris arrived wearing a flaming-red Gortex rain jacket, followed by two police cars with sirens blaring. The Reddington police force had already been stretched to capacity with the chaos at the cave. With this new crime, the department was completely overextended.

"What's happened to my nice peaceful Hill Country town?" he asked. "We haven't had a murder in fifteen years until Earth Pharm rolled into town. Now I have two in one night?"

He left them in the rain and went inside with one man. Zach, Max and Michael sat on the patio with the other officers to wait. Harris came back out moments later, his expression grim. He talked to his men, seeming not to care that Max, Zach and Michael overheard everything.

"Earlier this morning I called the crime-scene guys from Austin to help with Carl Madden's murder. They're already en route to Reddington. We're gonna have them process the body here first. I'm not taking a chance of contaminating the scene. This is beyond our expertise. Austin should be here within the hour.

"Meanwhile we need to set up a perimeter, start talking to neighbors." He assigned tasks to the officers and they dispersed to various parts of the property and neighborhood.

"My, my. Trouble does seem to follow you folks around." Heedless of the rain, Harris plopped down in one of the other chairs on the patio.

"You think the murders are related," said Max. It was a statement, not a question.

"On the record, I'm not supposed to speculate until we've investigated. Off the record. I'd bet my pension that we're dealing with same individual who killed Carl Madden."

"But why kill Ellen? Who would do this?" persisted Max.

"Someone who doesn't want you to get the answers you need when you go back down into Devil's Hollow," said Zach. "Someone who doesn't want the Earth Pharm project to succeed."

"That's what I don't understand," said Harris. "Who knows about the real research? Even Carl Madden thought it was about diamonds, not bacteria."

"I don't know where the diamond rumor is coming from," said Max. "We needed Ellen to tell us how to duplicate her bacteria lab results outside the cave. We're running into a significant problem."

"But how would anyone know about your problem?" asked Harris.

"They wouldn't necessarily have to know about that," said Zach. "Everyone in town knows Ellen was part of the initial team that found Devil's Hollow."

"And they knew she was a biochem student doing course work there in the cave this past spring," said Michael, "even if they didn't understand what it was about."

"So it could be anyone—from your team members to Joe over at the Gas N' Go. Not a lot of help, guys."

Harris hunkered down in his fiery-colored jacket and ignored their questioning looks. "I need to talk to you all individually. We could do it down at the station, but I can't leave here while I'm waiting on the CSI team. I'll speak to Dr. O'Neil first, then each of you one-on-one."

Max didn't want to be left alone, even with Harris. Zach and Michael looked like they wanted to argue, but stood up and walked out into the yard leaving her with the umbrella. Max felt distinctly uncomfortable—cold and prickly all over.

Harris didn't waste time on small talk; he got right down to business. "How well do you know the men on your team?" he asked.

"I've known them for at least two years. But you don't think that— Why, there's no way any of them could—" She stopped talking.

"What?"

"Well, I just realized I'm not a great judge of character— I mean…" This was mortifying, so she was glad Zach and Michael weren't there to hear it. "My ex-fiancé was having an affair for several months and I never suspected a thing. I don't know that I'm the best one to be asking that question."

She regarded the shrubbery at the edge of the yard for a moment. She'd grown up with staunch Presbyterian parents,

but imagined Catholic confession to be somewhat like talking
to Harris. "Tim Ryan has been in my lab for two years. Since
he's in the hospital, I'm not even considering him."

"Fair enough, for now."

"Sal Evans I've known for what feels like forever. We
worked together at PharmaVax before Earth Pharm. I don't
know much about Sal's personal life. He keeps to himself, but
I don't find that mysterious. I believe he's just a private person."

"Does he gamble?"

"Pardon me?"

"I'm trying to figure out if he could have any cash problems."

She thought for a moment, truly considering. "He likes to
bet on football and occasionally I hear about trips to Vegas."

"That's interesting." He shrugged and stretched at the same
time. "Doesn't mean anything other than the man likes black-
jack, but it's interesting. What about Martin?"

"I probably know Rodger least of all. He's amazing with
the lab equipment. Married. Has a couple of kids."

"Okay." Harris glanced at the two men in the side yard who
were unabashedly glaring back. Max was warmed by their
protectiveness. "I have to ask you about Michael and Zach."

She met the sheriff's gaze head-on. "Well, obviously I
just met them."

"Right. Which one do you have the more intimate relationship with?"

"Pardon me?" She heard her own voice rise in surprise.

"Well, it seems to me that they are both mighty solicitous,
so I want to make sure I understand the nature of the relationship between the three of you."

"The three of us? But you were in my room this morni—"
She stifled a laugh. It seemed horribly inappropriate under the
circumstances. "Oh my God. You thought all three of us were...
Oh, I see." Max smiled for the first time in what felt like forever.

Harris blushed all over his bald head.

"Sheriff, you have a terribly inflated opinion of my abilities. No, Michael is a business associate. My relationship with Zach Douglas is somewhat more…" Well, how the hell *did* she describe it? "Um…complicated."

Harris continued to burn scarlet. Looking at him, she was feeling a lot better about her tendency to flush from her scalp to her toes.

"Where was Michael during your confrontation with Carl Madden? Did you see him after you spoke with Madden in the living room?"

Max considered a moment. "I think he was in the common living area when Madden was there. I'm sorry, I really don't remember. I was exhausted at that point yesterday."

"And Zach?"

"We covered that earlier this morning, didn't we?"

"Yes, but I'd like to hear it again without him here."

Max exhaled loudly as sirens blared in the distance. The Austin team was arriving even sooner than Harris expected.

"Zach was with me all last night. There's no way he could have left long enough to do this. I can't imagine him doing it, anyway."

Harris nodded. "Folks in your situation rarely can."

She ignored the spurt of irritation.

Harris stood. The interview was over because his CSI team was here. "Okay. That's all I need for now. I'll catch up with Zach and Michael at the Lodge."

"Sheriff, we absolutely must get back into the cave."

"I don't believe that'll be possible. The cavern entrance is part of a double-homicide investigation. The scene is still being processed." He turned to leave.

She reached for his arm but stopped herself. "If we don't get back down there, the pond will flood and Ellen's death will be meaningless. I beg you. Let us get some answers. Ellen's life has to stand for something." She searched his face. Surely he wasn't going to insist on procedure and let this opportunity pass the world by.

The man nodded, but he wasn't paying attention to her or agreeing to anything. He was distracted by the crime-scene team's arrival. He started toward the approaching vehicles before turning back and fixing her with a steely gaze.

"This—" he pointed to Ellen's house "—changes everything. I'll talk with Zach and Kirk later, but I don't see how it can possibly happen tonight."

Max hadn't thought she could feel any worse. But she'd been wrong. Her sense of hopelessness grew as she watched him walk over to greet the officers pulling up to the duplex. Michael and Zach joined her when the crime-scene officers unloaded from the black-and-white police van.

"So?" asked Michael.

"You wouldn't believe me if I told you," she said.

"Oh, I've had several things stretch my reality meter today," Michael said morosely. "Try me."

Max recalled Harris's inferences about their relationship, glanced at Zach and shook her head. "No, trust me. I'm not going there. And Harris isn't going to let us back in the cavern. He said he'd talk with Zach and Kirk later, but I'm pretty sure we're locked out." She watched the house and the officers walking in and out of the sliding-glass door.

"I have no idea what we're going to do about collecting the specimens." Voicing that fear aloud made it even scarier. "I know it's wretched to think about the samples at this point, but right now that's all I can focus on that will make any of this make sense. I can't even cry for Ellen, I feel so numb."

Zach's face was unfathomable. He stared at the glass door. "Excuse me a minute, I've got to speak with Harris." He walked to the slider and talked with an officer. Seconds later Harris appeared on the threshold and Zach stepped inside.

"Don't worry," said Michael. "Kirk and his checkbook will get us back into Devil's Hollow, you'll see."

Max felt vaguely nauseated. She wasn't so sure.

Zach reappeared less than five minutes later. "Let's head

to the Lodge and figure out how you're going to prepare those specimen jars."

"What did Harris say?" asked Max.

He looked at her, his eyes still unreadable.

"'We'll see.' That's a direct quote."

"Same thing he told me."

"We need to be ready just in case though, right?" said Zach.

"Right." She stood, trying to be optimistic but swaying a bit on her feet. Zach grabbed her arm to steady her.

"Still numb," she muttered.

He slid a comforting arm around her shoulders. She looked up expecting encouragement; his eyes were bleak.

"It's okay," he said. "Be grateful you're numb right now. The feelings will come. But you don't really want them. Trust me."

# Chapter Seventeen

Zach kept his arm around Max all the way home. He held her hand until they reached the front door of the Lodge where Rodger and Sal met them. They'd gotten word about Ellen. In small towns news really did travel fast. Max missed the warmth of Zach's fingers as soon as he dropped her hand.

"I'm really sorry," said Sal. "I don't know what else to say."

"There are no words," said Zach. "Not really."

Rodger nodded.

Michael didn't even stop to speak. He just headed to his room; he was in bad shape. Zach headed upstairs, too. He'd gotten steadily quieter on the trip back to the Lodge, despite taking care of Max.

Max desperately wanted to follow Zach up to the room and change into dry clothes, but Rodger and Sal wanted to talk. To process everything that had happened. And they had news.

Mrs. Mabry was clearing the sideboard and offered to make more fresh coffee. Max reluctantly agreed.

Rodger and Sal had all of Kirk's new lab equipment spread out on the dining table. "We've got it, Max. We got it." Sal was trying to be deferential to the sad news they'd just received, but his eyes glowed with repressed excitement.

She set down the fresh coffee and attempted to switch gears. "What? How?" she asked.

"Kirk called his friend, Ellen's Professor Weatheridge, before we heard about what had happened." Rodger held up a sheaf of papers. "The guy faxed over Ellen's lab notes from the original project. He still had them in his office. Unbelievable luck. You know how college profs are, they never throw anything away."

"Guess how she did it, Max. Guess." Sal was like a kid with a new bicycle, so excited he couldn't give her time to answer. "We weren't that far off. It's a protein bath, not a chemical bath. That was the difference." It took a moment for the implication to sink in.

"Oh, I get it now." She felt the first flicker of optimism since she'd plopped into the wet chair on Ellen's broken patio.

Sal showed her the specimen bottles they were prepping. "We're doing a dozen of them. We have the exact specifications here." Sal pointed to the pages.

"Perfect." Max held on to a glimmer of hope.

"We're doing a couple of chemical baths, too, just to experiment with."

"Great, great. Where's Kirk?" Now she had to speak to him before she could change.

"Upstairs. I think he's been on the phone with the sheriff."

Max headed up and knocked on Kirk's door.

"Come in, Max." His voice wasn't at its normal booming tone. "Hello, darlin', you okay?"

She took a deep breath and started talking before she was all the way inside. "No. Yes. Hell, I don't know. It was horrible. I'm numb. Zach told me I should be grateful for that. I think I will be for n—" She stopped when she saw Zach standing beside the door. She hadn't realized he was there.

With the loss of his daughter and his wife, Kirk knew a bit about wanting the pain of loss to be numbed. He picked up the conversation as if there'd been no interruption. "For now that's good advice. You've got work to do. Work that will make Miss Garrett's death mean something more than just a hideous tragedy."

Max was staring, unsure how she felt about Zach being in the room. Her numbness seemed to have extended to several different areas.

"Do you have the equipment ready?" Kirk asked.

She nodded vaguely. "Rodger and Sal are finishing up downstairs."

"Excellent," said Kirk. "I believe Mrs. Mabry is going to feed us before we go. Zach and Michael are going out early. We'll be there later with Don."

"Wh-what happened? Is Harris going to let us in?" asked Max.

"Why don't you ask Zach?"

"What's going on?" asked Max, blinking to clear the cobwebs and picking up on the tension in the room. Kirk was glaring a hole through him. This was not a friendly meeting.

"Interesting negotiating skills your boyfriend has."

"I don't understand. Quit being dramatic and tell me what's happening here."

"Nothing really. We just have a pirate as our cavern guide." Kirk wasn't smiling.

Zach spoke up for the first time. "Kirk, this is better for Earth Pharm. Better for the city. Hell, it's even better for Harris long-term. And no laws are being broken. You said so yourself. This will make Ellen's death mean something."

"Right, well, it's going to cost a bit more than I expected."

"Close your eyes and think of the PR." There was no hiding the antipathy in his voice. "That should get you through." Zach slipped out of the room.

"What the hell is going on?" demanded Max again.

Kirk scowled at the closing door. "We're going into the cavern at ten-thirty tonight."

"And?"

"And Earth Pharm is building a Wellness Clinic here in Reddington after this is all over. Probably something that will be dedicated to Ellen Garrett."

It took her a moment to put it together. Zach had gone back in to speak with Harris before they left Ellen's duplex. "That's how this is all coming about?"

"Yes," said Kirk. "We just hashed out some of the details by phone. It's going to cost the company a fortune, but—" He looked at the door thoughtfully. "This is a poor community. Harris couldn't exactly say no."

She was stunned. In the midst of the shock and grief over Ellen, Zach had thought through that much of the process. Max had been sitting in a puddle of water trying not to throw up while he'd been salvaging their project. "It's an excellent idea," she murmured.

"Could be. Zach didn't like the idea of an overt political bribe to Harris's campaign. He told me we needed to invest in the area." Kirk shook his head. "It's all about semantics, but…" He stopped and looked at her, really looked at her. "Max, we need to talk."

She didn't want to talk, but Kirk was stubborn and he was going to insist. Max had a distinct sense of déjà vu as she sat in her mentor's room, the scent of his ever-present Darjeeling tea perfuming the air.

"You're a scientist," he began. "You know we're a paranoid bunch. We suspect everyone. Don't trust anyone."

She regarded him with surprise. He was practically repeating her conversation with Zach word for word. "I tried to tell…"

"What?" he asked.

Kirk studied her with a curiosity that had Max backpedaling at warp speed. She could share many things with her mentor, but not her relationship with Zach.

"I suppose we are inordinately paranoid," she admitted.

"Well, I am, and I'm not too proud to admit it. Especially where those I care about are concerned." Kirk opened a bag beside his chair. "That's why I want you to have this." He pulled out a small rectangular case and Max's stomach roiled.

"What is that?"

"It's exactly what you think it is."

"I don't need a gun."

"Darlin', you know how I hate to contradict you."

She raised a skeptical eyebrow. They both knew the exact opposite. He loved to contradict her.

"But you absolutely do need this," he insisted. "Too much is unknown here. You're going into the cave tonight. And just like Sal and Rodger figured out multiple ways of prepping those specimen jars, I want you to have multiple ways of protecting yourself."

"But I already have a bodyguard. Zach is here, I'll—"

Kirk interrupted. "We have no idea who is out to stop us from succeeding or what their motivations are. Zach is one line of defense, that's true. And I think he can be trusted.

"This—" he held up the gun case "—is plan B. You're an excellent shot. I taught you myself. Our project has ramifications that are too far-reaching to trust this will all just go away. I don't want you unable to protect yourself against people you can supposedly trust."

"What are you saying?" she asked.

"I'm saying, don't trust anyone down there but yourself." He opened the case. Inside was a small handgun.

Max's head spun from the idea that Kirk wasn't one hundred percent on board with trusting Zach. Was there anyone he believed in absolutely?

"I trust him, Kirk. I don't care if you do think he's a pirate." She tried to joke, but the words surprised her, even as they left her lips. She hadn't thought she was going to have this conversation.

He stopped his perusal of the handgun. "Why? Because you've slept with him? Darlin', you know a man is never more creative with the truth than when he's trying to get a woman into bed."

Max shook her head. "No, that's not why I trust him. I—" She blew out a breath. Okay, she definitely wasn't going to discuss *this* with him.

Kirk wasn't her father or her best friend, and it wasn't appropriate to talk about her sex life here. But she realized she did trust Zach and that was something she hadn't been sure of until Kirk had called it into question just now.

"How did you get on the airplane with this?" She forced herself to pick up the gun even as she tried to divert the conversation.

"Who says I got on the airplane with it?" He winked and flashed his infuriating Kirk grin. "We all have our secrets."

"Kirk—"

"No arguing. I want you to take it. I can't handle the thought of you unprotected down there."

She looked at him. There was no way he was going to take no for an answer. Not about this. "All right." She checked the barrel and the safety before slipping it back into the case. "Because you're asking me to, not because I think I need it."

"Understood. Now, how about one more cup of tea?"

"No, I'm going to change out of these wet clothes."

He looked a bit sad, like he wanted to say something but didn't. "Of course. I'll see you at dinner."

He gave her a look that told her he knew she was going to do more than change. She ignored that and simply nodded on the way out the door. She wasn't thinking about food; she had to get to Zach.

She'd realized something else while talking to Kirk. Zach had a need to protect her just like her mentor did and she hadn't been willing to let either of them close enough to do it.

Zach needed to know she understood how he felt. Not that she would let that interfere with her work, but showing him as well as telling him she trusted him and understood him suddenly seemed enormously important.

MAX HURRIED down the hall to their room. Funny, she didn't mind thinking of it that way anymore. The shower was running as she unlocked the door. She remembered this morning, a hundred years ago, and was out of her T-shirt and toeing off her tennis shoes before she could reconsider. Right now, nothing was more important than her being in that shower with Zach.

The bathroom was humid and steamy, the mirror completely fogged over. She wasn't being particularly quiet as she stripped naked, but ripping back the shower curtain didn't feel right, either. She had a moment of uncertainty. Before she completely lost her nerve, she pulled part of the vinyl curtain away.

Steam poured out of the enclosure. Zach's back was to her, his powerful shoulders shaking. The grief was palpable. Water pummeled his upper back, running down his well-defined body like tears.

Her heart ached for his pain and loss. She hesitated as all her plans washed away with the water running down the drain. Did she leave him in peace or stay to offer comfort?

This seemed too personal. Too private.

She was about to drop the curtain when he turned. His face was filled with such profound sadness. Water beat down on his chest from the showerhead. His eyes were red from crying and he looked so…lost. He shook his head and started to pivot away.

She remembered his comment to Rodger and Sal from downstairs.

*There are no words*.

In the end, none were necessary. She simply stepped inside the spray and pulled him into her arms.

# *Chapter Eighteen*

Three hours later Max was eating a sandwich and looking at the specimen bottles Rodger and Sal had prepared. She'd missed supper and woken up in bed alone. Zach was long gone. Apparently he'd left with Michael for the cavern while she was sleeping.

That nagged at her. He hadn't talked to her after they'd made love. He'd held her close until she'd fallen asleep in his arms and then left without saying goodbye.

It was ridiculous for her to feel snubbed. He probably just needed some space after coming apart earlier. She was going to see him in a couple of hours. But still, his leaving without saying goodbye felt very…final.

"So you think this will work?" asked Sal. His voice snapped her back to the present.

Max looked up from the tiny jars she'd been staring at. "I do. We've got two chemical and ten protein baths here. One of them is bound to work." She crossed her fingers as they sorted the plastic bottles into her green daypack. Kirk's gun case was hidden on the bottom.

"Once we're at the pool we'll make sure to get the pH, temperature, alkalinity and electrical conductivity readings so we can reproduce the conditions. We'll bring out some of the rocks from the pond, too."

"Right."

Kirk helped pack the other equipment. "Harris wants us out of the cavern before sunrise," he announced. "We'd better get going."

Mrs. Mabry had made sandwiches earlier, but was gone for the evening. The house felt strangely deserted as they loaded up. Sal, Rodger and Kirk all piled into the Grand Cherokee along with Max. The rain stopped while Don drove them out to Devil's Hollow.

When they arrived just after ten there was a small crowd of people at the barricade. The officer on duty started to wave their Jeep away, but Kirk got out and spoke to him. After a short discussion on his radio, the policeman waved them through.

Max took a deep breath and willed away her nervousness and headache. She would not put up with a migraine or claustrophobia right now. There wasn't room in her life for those weaknesses tonight. It was time.

ZACH STOOD AT THE mouth of Devil's Hollow. How in the hell was he going to do this? Max would never forgive him, but there was no way she was going back down into that cavern. Not after yesterday's near-disaster and Ellen's murder today.

While he was overwhelmed and grateful to Max for putting him back together tonight, he wasn't going to risk her life in the cave again. As for this evening, he wasn't sure why she'd done it. Was it pity or was she "taking one for the team"?

Didn't really matter. Once he refused to let her go into the caverns, she'd never speak to him again, much less go to bed with him. He only hoped that Kirk would back him up on the staying-above-ground issue.

"Michael, you got all the ropes ready?"

"Yeah, as soon as we're clear, I'll drop 'em in."

Sheriff Harris walked over to where Michael and Zach were reviewing the final details. "I just got word on the radio.

Your group is coming up from the outer barricades. I'm sending these guards on break for thirty minutes. Is that enough time for you to get down?"

"Yes," said Zach. "That should be plenty. Thank you, Harris. You won't be sorry."

"That remains to be seen. Just remember. If this goes south, I was never here and my men never saw you and Michael with this equipment."

Zach nodded.

Harris and his men filed into a Reddington police van and drove away, leaving Michael and Zach alone at the entrance. The Jeep from the Lodge pulled to a stop in almost the same spot. Everyone piled out with their packs. Zach sucked in a deep gulp of air. It was time.

When Max spotted him, she smiled. Zach felt his body's own automatic response and called himself three kinds of fool. Had she finally come around to trusting him? Or, as he feared, did she just need him intact to guide their group?

She'd said earlier she couldn't let go of control on this project because it was too important. That conversation worried him so much he'd left her sleeping in their bed instead of waking her tonight.

"Hey, guys, the gear is over there," said Zach. Michael was already setting up a couple of lanterns by the overhang entrance and pulling equipment out of the duffels.

"Max, I need to ask you about something." Zach didn't give her a chance to answer. He simply took her by the arm away from the others. "We need to talk." That sounded ominous even to his own ears.

"What is it?" Her eyes were bright. Despite everything, she was excited about going back into Devil's Hollow.

He took a deep breath. "Max, you can't go inside."

"What? What do you mean I can't go?"

"I mean, you're not going into the cavern tonight. Not after what happened yesterday with—" he looked around to make sure they couldn't be overheard "—the headaches and the auras. It's too dangerous. If that were to happen while we were climbing, you could get yourself or someone else killed. You're staying topside."

Her face changed, going from open trust to surprise, hurt, then fury.

"The hell I am. I'm in charge of this project and you've been trying to take it away from me from the beginning. I...I can't trust you, can I?"

She spat the words at him, her angry eyes shimmering with unshed tears. This was what he'd needed to happen, to get her so mad she would hardly speak to him. Anything to keep her out of the cave. As she scrubbed a hand across her face and turned away, a shot rang out, striking the rock where she'd been standing. It ricocheted, sending shards of rock into the air. Max pivoted back toward the sound. She obviously didn't realize what it was.

"Get down!" Zach didn't take time to explain. He simply tackled her from behind and shouted to the others, "Someone's shooting at us!"

He hit the ground first and rolled so Max landed on top of him instead of the bedrock. His hip connected with a sharp edge of stone as they fell behind an outcropping of rock.

More shots rang out. They were protected by a smaller overhang, but not if the shooter had an infrared device or if he changed position.

Zach took a minute to catch his breath. Max landing on his chest had knocked the wind from his lungs. "Are you all right?" she asked.

Zach nodded.

"Everyone okay?" he called, his breath still coming out as a thin wheeze.

"We're all together. We're okay," called Michael. "We're under the big overhang."

"What do we do?" asked Max.

"We're targets out here in the open. We've gotta get to the entrance without getting shot. Give me a minute." Zach crouched behind their hiding place. He couldn't see anything and their lanterns made them a beacon.

This was bad. The Sheriff was gone for the next thirty minutes. None of them had a gun. They were sitting ducks if they couldn't get to the car. As he assessed the situation, another hail of bullets rained down.

He pulled Max underneath him to shield her, but the shots weren't directed at them. The sound was that of metal being struck. The shooter was aiming for the Grand Cherokee. If the Jeep was disabled, they were effectively stranded.

Gunshots continued to pop against metal with a carnival-like unreality as Zach pulled Max to her feet and they raced toward the safety of the cave's rock overhang. His hip slowed him down, but they made it just as the shooter finished with the Jeep. The sound of steam escaping the radiator was the death knell for any idea of leaving the area by car.

"So what do you think?" asked Michael.

Zach looked around at the group. No one was too much the worse for wear, but they weren't one hundred percent, either. Sal had twisted his ankle getting to the overhang and Rodger had a nasty gash on his forearm. Kirk's head wound had opened up again. Don was the only one who hadn't been banged up in some way.

"There's nowhere to go but down into the cavern," said Zach. The argument from moments ago with Max was forgotten. "Michael, how long will it take us to get the harnesses together to get down there?"

"The ropes are ready. It's just a matter of getting all the other equipment out, strapping everyone in and going."

"Sounds like a plan." Zach opened the largest duffel and pulled out the harnesses as Michael and Don started gearing everyone up.

Max pulled the small pack off her shoulders and dove into

it. Zach wasn't really paying attention to what she was looking for. He grabbed a pack filled with food, water and first-aid supplies and handed it off to Don.

"Michael, you and Don will be first in and belay the rest of the group. I'll stay topside to get everyone else down."

"With the guy shooting at us, how are we going to get into the cave?" asked Sal.

"With this." Max finished rummaging in her pack and tossed it aside. She held a Glock at shoulder level.

"Where did that come from?" asked Zach.

"Where do you think?" snapped Kirk. "She's an excellent shot. I taught her myself. She's better than me, and you know I'm not humble."

Max nodded. "I can provide cover or at least distract the shooter."

"I don't know—" Zach began.

"I'll take what I can get," said Michael.

The others agreed.

Zach knew immediately he was outnumbered, but he still didn't like it.

The cavern entrance was partially protected by the large overhang, but they had to be careful because the shooter could have moved while they'd been regrouping. They decided Max would huddle in front under the edge of the overhang and cover the folks descending by firing just before they were exposed.

Before Michael and Don ducked out to the entrance, Max fired in the direction of the last shots. All clear. Then Rodger and Sal stepped out. They had just started down when more gunfire rang out. Everyone ducked. Rodger and Sal were safely below the surface before a new round of bullets came, but the angle of the shots indicated that the shooter had indeed changed positions.

Kirk was next. Max repeated the procedure and just as he sank beneath the surface, another shot came from a different angle. The slug ricocheted off rock and shards of stone splintered into the cavern opening. Zach heard shouts from below; the rope went taut.

"Kirk, you okay?" Max shouted and tried to get to the edge, but Zach shooed her back to the cover of the overhang.

"I can see him. He didn't fall." Zach lay flat on his belly in the shelter of the rock, trying to make himself as small a target as possible.

"Is he hit?" Max called.

"I can't tell."

The lights from the lanterns danced along the jagged walls of the tunnel. Zach could see Kirk. He was upright with one arm dangling at his side. Michael unhooked him from the descender and called up to Zach, "Off rope."

Zach pulled the rope and ducked under the overhang. Shots hit the rock face behind them. The gunman had moved again.

"We've gotta get out of here now," he said.

"What about Kirk?"

Zach didn't know the answer, so he didn't meet her gaze as he pulled on his backpack of equipment. They had to get away and if he stopped to explain all this, it could slow them down. He couldn't afford that. It was too dangerous.

"Answer me, Zach."

He rifled through the pile of gear until he found her fluorescent green pack. Without speaking, he slid it onto her shoulders and grabbed her hand. He pulled her to the edge of the opening, keeping as low a profile as possible.

"Is Kirk okay?" she demanded. Fear made her voice quiver as he clipped her harness on to the rope and the descender.

"Put the gun away, Max." This time he met her eyes. "Let's go find out."

# Chapter Nineteen

Max's feet hit the ground with a jarring thud. She hadn't been able to really control her descent between the shooter above and her worry about Kirk. Her heart rate skyrocketed as she unclipped the carabiner from her harness, but it had nothing to do with rappelling into the cave. She hadn't even thought about her fear of heights.

Don and Michael were wearing helmets with lanterns. The lights threw crazy shadows on the wall. The rest of the team was gone.

"They've moved into the larger chamber beyond. It'd be like shooting fish in a barrel if we just sat down here at the bottom," said Michael.

She shuddered at the picture that presented. "Right." Don handed her a helmet and she headed for the large opening in the floor.

She wouldn't fit with the backpack on, so she had to push it through ahead of herself. When she slipped it from her shoulders, she realized Zach had taken extra time to find her own pack with the specimen jars inside while they were being shot at. In the midst of the chaos, no matter what he'd said earlier, some part of him must believe they could get her samples.

Suddenly he was there behind her and she was staring at the pack. If she hadn't already decided that he was not for her, she would really be in trouble here. She might have fallen a little in love with him over that.

The light from his helmet shone in her face as she just stood there and looked up at him. His eyes were shadowed, but something unspoken passed between them. She wanted to reach out and touch him, to thank him, but—

"Come on, Max. Let's go."

She found her voice. "What about Don and Michael?"

"They're pulling the ropes so the shooter can't follow on our own lines. They'll be right behind us."

The moment was gone, so she turned to move through the long crawl space into the larger room ahead. She took a deep breath before going in, her claustrophobia beaten back for the moment by sheer panic.

At the end of the tube she found a small triage unit set up. Kirk was in the center of the activity. The soft rumble of the waterfall was a soothing background noise after the harsh sound of gunfire above. Everyone's lights reflecting off the walls gave the impression of a dimly lit room.

"Son of a bitch, how in holy hell am I supposed to hold still when you're shoving a freaking spike into my shoulder?"

A wave of relief coursed through her. A cussing Kirk was a breathing Kirk.

"We've got to stop the bleeding," said Sal. "I'm sorry, sir." Rodger and Sal were standing on either side of him, and as she approached he began using curse words in combinations Max had honestly never heard or considered before.

Kirk looked at her through pain-glazed eyes. Blood covered his face and shirt. She wasn't sure if his head wound from earlier had opened up due to ricocheting rock or if the blood was from a new injury.

"I got shot. They say it went straight through my arm. So that's a good thing, right?" He smiled despite the pain. "Dr. Death here is patching me up."

Max sat on the rock floor beside her mentor and took his

uninjured hand. His fingers were cold. "That's a rather offensive thing to say to the man who is taking care of you," she teased softly.

Sal shrugged. "No offense taken."

"Well, I'm glad the real EMT is here." Kirk looked up at Zach with obvious relief. "You got a first-aid kit in any of those packs? You knocked me on my ass last time. Surely you can fix this?"

Max glanced at Zach in surprise.

"Michael does. He's right behind us." Zach pulled his pack open and turned to Sal. "Good job using your T-shirts to stem the blood flow. I'd have done the same." He started working on Kirk.

Sal sank to the cavern floor beside Rodger and took off his boot. His ankle was three times its normal size. Rodger's arm dangled at an odd angle. Blood oozed from a gash on the back of his arm, too.

Zach glanced over his shoulder at them. "Looks like you two could use some help, as well."

"We'll wait our turn," said Rodger.

Michael arrived with the full first-aid kit and his hand wrapped in a bandanna.

"What happened?" asked Max.

"Murphy's Law. The clip jammed and caught my finger when we were pulling it. Just a bad pinch is all."

"Let me see." Max stood. Michael's hand was dripping blood. "You need stitches," she said.

"Zach can do it."

She shook her head. Was there anything Zach couldn't do? "Where's Don?" she asked.

"He's a lookout at the mouth of the cave. Just in case our shooter starts down, we'll have some warning." Michael lifted his hand above his shoulder to slow the blood flow. "They'll have to set their own ropes, so we'll know a few minutes beforehand."

"Good plan," said Zach.

"What do we do now?" asked Max.

Zach examined Rodger's arm. "Harris will be back soon."

"Can't we just call up to them and get out?" Sal moved around, like he was trying to get his ankle in a comfortable position.

"Yes, and till then, we need to sit tight, right here," said Zach.

"No more gunfire to contend with," agreed Kirk.

"But while we're here…" began Max. "For what I'm sure is the last time we'll be allowed to be inside…" She was still having a hard time saying this and she wasn't sure why. It was what she wanted more than anything. To go and find the bacteria. To make her mark in the scientific world with this discovery. To find the cure.

"Yes?" asked Zach.

"I don't want to just wait. I want to go and get the samples from the pond. It'll be flooded the next time they let us come back down here."

Everyone seemed to be holding their breath except her boss.

Zach looked at her and the people around them. He had to buy into this. He was the only one who could take her to the pond, given everyone else's injuries save Don. But Don could get these folks out when the time came.

*I'll leave my gun with Michael and Don.*

"No, you can leave them my gun," Kirk whispered.

"What? Are you a mind reader now?" asked Max.

"Only where you're concerned. That was written all over your face. My Ruger is in that blue pack." Kirk pointed it out on the floor. "I couldn't get to it topside before you were pulling out your Glock like Annie Oakley. You didn't think you were the only one coming down here armed, did you?"

She had to laugh to keep from crying. "Kirk, you are insane."

"Oh, I've been called worse," he whispered. "And by you, too. I've also—" He hesitated, looked up, and Max followed his gaze. He was watching Zach.

"Kirk, what is it?" she murmured.

"Ah, nothing. We just need to have that pot of tea when we get out of here. And you'll tell me all about your latest Toby mug acquisition. All right, darlin'?"

She smiled and gave in to the urge to kiss his forehead. "Of course."

Zach nodded his head at them. "You're both crazy. Apparently, I am, too."

What did he mean? Would he help her? She stared at him, unwilling to look away. Zach had made no secret he thought this whole project was a huge lie. That Max herself had lied to him, as well. But she'd forgotten about the others she was dealing with. Kirk, Sal and Rodger wanted her to succeed almost as much as she did herself. Zach knew it, too.

"What do you absolutely have to take with you to the pool?" Zach asked. "And I'm not talking about guns."

ZACH ANCHORED the nylon rope to a boulder and tossed the coiled line into the fissure before him. He clipped in with his harness and slowly began the descent into the pit. This might be the biggest risk he'd ever taken—in his personal life and in his caving career. That they were happening simultaneously was just fate's way of kicking him in the ass when he was down. What in the world had he been thinking?

Hell, he knew what he'd been thinking. Max wrapped around him this morning and again tonight in the shower. He'd been grateful and hoping for a chance to repeat the experiences. He'd also been feeling the pressure of all those hopes and dreams in the cavern room a few moments ago.

That waterfall chamber was huge, but he'd felt he was suffocating in a closet with four pairs of eyes turned on him, yearning for something that he alone was responsible for delivering. He hated the thought of that. Hated it.

Part of the cost of believing, he reasoned.

So here he was, leading Max deeper into a flooding cave toward a pool that might or might not already be underwater to gather some samples that might or might not cure the scourge of the modern world, all while someone was trying to kill them. Just another typical day at the office.

He almost laughed. He had to or he just might run screaming down one of the offshoot tunnels they'd passed earlier on the way to the pond.

They got to the bridge where Tim had had his close encounter with mortality and crossed it without incident. Zach held on to Max as they walked the narrow path. Her breathing quickened, but other than that she gave no indication she was nervous. They didn't talk much. Each was lost in their own thoughts.

The constant sound of water was the only noise. That and their feet on the rocks. This suited Zach fine. He was concerned about what he might tell her if he started talking right now. They took a break after the bridge to drink and eat a Clif bar. They'd been walking for an hour and a half.

"We're close," said Zach.

"Good," breathed Max. "The air feels heavier."

"It's the humidity. The water is definitely rising. Can you hear it?" There was a deeper rumbling sound, like the waterfall back at the entry. It was getting louder, echoing off the cave walls. They were close.

"That's not a good sign, is it?"

He shook his head.

Moments later, they rounded the corner leading to the pool and ran into a wall of rock. Tons of it covered the path to the pond. "Rockslide." Zach swore. "Probably from yesterday's explosion, or the rising water, or a combination of the two."

Shining their headlamps through the debris, they could see the water about forty yards away, but they couldn't reach it. Calling it quits wasn't an option. Instead, they backtracked and took an offshoot tunnel, gambling they could get to the water from there.

They had to climb up and rappel down. It took an hour.

Once at the bottom of the wall, they were again within sight of the pond. Miraculously the rockslide stopped fifty feet from the water and the pool was unscathed. Max began unloading her supplies. Zach hiked down into the passageway below the pond, where he'd been just the day before.

He took a flashlight from his pack and directed it toward the end of the corridor. What he found surprised him. At his feet, water lapped softly against the rock where yesterday there had been nothing but a gravel path. His homemade marker was long gone. Farther out his light reflected off water rushing past in the main passageway. The flooding aquifer had made a new set of streams inside the cavern corridors.

He made his way back to Max. She was up at the pool carefully unloading her supplies and specimen bottles.

"You made a good call," he said.

"What?"

"The water's almost here."

She stopped for a moment. "How long do we have?"

"An hour at the most."

"That's enough time," she said. "But I'm going to need your help."

"What can I do?"

"First we have to collect these samples." She'd pulled almost a dozen plastic specimen jars from her pack. "We get the samples first just in case we have any contamination in the measuring process."

"Right."

She showed him how to glove up and use the syringes to collect the bacteria. Together they filled each of the bottles and lined them up neatly along the rock bank. She also collected some rock samples from the shoreline of the pond.

"Okay, what's next?" he asked.

She pulled out a notebook and a complicated little meter. "Now we have to measure the room temp, alkalinity, pH, water temp and electrical conductivity of the water."

"How about you take the measurements and I record your readings?"

"Right."

Zach wrote everything she said in her notebook, dutifully scribing the data she measured. She looked over his shoulder occasionally to make sure he got the notations so she would understand her own dictation. The water continued to rise. They could hear it, a steady *drip, drip*. But they were making steady progress, too. Zach enjoyed watching her in this light because she couldn't tell he was staring.

All the cavern's chambers were dark, but this one was especially so, even with their helmets' high-powered carbide lights. The dark-hued limestone seemed to swallow up all illumination. No refractions or shimmering sparkles reflected off the walls as in other areas of the cavern. The room was practically black.

That was probably why he hadn't seen it at first. They were packing up and readying to leave when he finally did. It was situated beside the pond. A small drum-shaped package. A miniature oil barrel, no bigger than five gallons. On top was a timer with lights that looked suspiciously like explosives.

"What the hell is that?" asked Max.

## Chapter Twenty

"What do you think it is?" asked Zach.

The light from Max's helmet shone on the drum. "It looks like a bomb of some kind."

"Yeah, that's what I'm thinking, too." Not that Zach had experience with bombs, but he'd watched enough television to know what he was looking at.

*Well, hell. How did that get here?*

He walked over to get a closer look and took out his flashlight to point the beam toward the small barrel.

"I wouldn't get too close if I were you." A disembodied voice came out of the darkness and the *drip, drip* of water turned to the steady shuffle of footsteps coming toward them. Zach swung his flashlight toward the sound. A woman's smirking face appeared.

"Mrs. Mabry?" murmured Max.

Yet it wasn't Mrs. Mabry. This looked like Mrs. Mabry's younger biker-chick sister. She was blond instead of brunette and she was a good deal leaner and meaner. That impression was helped by the 9mm SIG-Sauer P250 she was pointing at them.

"No, my dear Max, you can call me Marnie. Mrs. Mabry was just a cover. A good one, don't you think? Prosthetics and wigs are amazing. And I do make a mean breakfast muffin, don't I, Zach? It was my grandma's recipe."

The woman laughed. The sound was harsh and bounced off the cavern walls. "But my real specialty is baking of a different sort. The chemical explosive kind. That's why I'd encourage you to step away from that little barrel and get your hands up."

"Wh-what is going on? Why are you doing this?" asked Max. Her hands were in her pack.

"I know. You have lots of questions. If you could have just stayed away, everything would have been fine. Some days I really hate my job." She sneered. "Sorry, private joke." But no one was laughing. "I said get your hands up, Dr. O'Neil."

Max's hands stilled and she slowly brought them out of the pack at Zach's feet, raising them to her side.

"Why are you doing this?" asked Zach again. He pushed aside his astonishment and tried to come up with a plan. He had to keep Marnie talking.

"Simple. I work for folks who don't want a cancer cure to be found. Their companies have too much money invested in treating the disease. So I was hired to ensure that this 'cure' went away."

Max looked ill in the wash of the white light. But she couldn't be surprised. It was exactly what she'd told him was going on.

"My God. Why?" Max asked. "When people suffer and die needlessly?"

"Honey, it's not about the suffering, it's all about the money. Cancer treatment is an extraordinarily profitable business and right now it's more lucrative for the disease to exist as a scourge than it is to be cured."

"You're evil," said Max.

Marnie shook her head, seemingly not at all offended. "No, I'm a capitalist."

Zach's blood ran cold at the explanation. Marnie was echoing his words of yesterday. But this was so very different. It was PharmaVax times ten, willing to let hundreds of thousands die for profit. He couldn't think about the similarities to Tammy's situation or he and Max wouldn't survive.

Right now he had to focus on distracting Marnie. That was their only hope for getting out.

"How did you get in here?" he asked.

"Now, Zach, you didn't think you'd discovered the only entrance into Devil's Hollow, did you, dear?"

"What are you doing?" asked Max.

"Why, I'm destroying the pond, of course. With this little jewel—" she indicated the barrel "—as soon as it's detonated. It won't make a big boom like those idiots this afternoon. Although they almost did my job for me. But just enough to open the canister and spill the contents into the pool." She held a small rectangular box in her hand. It looked like a thick television remote. "I can do it from far away or from right here."

"What's in the canister?" asked Max.

"A superconcentrated organophosphate. It was developed as a nerve agent compound for the military."

Max went very still and tense beside him. "Why use something so toxic to destroy the pond?" she asked. "You could pour cooking oil in that pool and have the same result in terms of destroying the bacteria. Tainted water from here will eventually end up in the aquifer that supplies water for the entire lower half of the state. You could harm hundreds of people with an organophosphate nerve compound."

Marnie was quiet for a moment before she answered. "Remember, Dr. O'Neil, it's all about the money. Not about the suffering. Some of my investors have other interests besides direct pharmaceutical sales."

"Don't they realize you could be making some areas of the state uninhabitable that rely completely on the aquifer for water?" asked Max.

Marnie shrugged indifferently. "Not their problem, nor mine, either."

Zach swallowed hard against the bile rising in the back of his throat as he realized this committee was willing to kill thousands immediately to save their profits. "But you're talking about the ultimate in overkill," argued Zach, struggling to stay calm and keep the revulsion out of his voice. "This is more than stopping a cure from being found. It's creating a whole new major ecological and humanitarian disaster. With a nerve agent, thousands could become sick or even die."

Max had been moving closer to Zach as he'd been talking. When he finished speaking, she was standing beside him with one arm partially hidden. He glanced down and realized she'd been inching as close to her pack as possible, not to him. Marnie couldn't see this in the darkness. The whole conversation had taken on a surreal quality. He knew she was going for her Glock and there was no way to stop her without outing her.

"Like I said, not my problem. This is how my investors want it done. I'm all about the money. Now, we're wasting time." Her voice was sharp. "And I can't see you. Move out from behind him."

"Wait," said Max, moving directly to Zach's side and into Marnie's line of sight. "Why did you start the rumor about the diamonds?"

"Why do you think? I had to slow you down. Nothing better than greed to confuse the issue with the good citizens of Reddington."

"But why kill Carl Madden?" asked Zach.

The woman sighed, obviously impatient to get on with her business. Zach ignored her nonverbal cues. *Keep talking, Marnie.*

"And Ellen Garrett? If you knew you were going to do this—" he inclined his head toward the pond "—why did you have to kill her?" He hoped Marnie's ego would keep her distracted with trying to justify her behavior.

"We had to know that there were no other samples above ground. I only intended to question Ellen. But she panicked and then there was nothing to do but—"

Zach didn't think the woman was going to say anything

else until she cleared her throat. "Now, we have to get on with this. I can't leave you down here ~~as loose ends~~. It's obvious that you and Max can't be trusted to stay out of my plans. But once the compound destroys the pond, it doesn't matter what you do. Zach, you're first." She tossed the rope at Max, but Zach caught it.

He passed the smooth nylon line to Max, squeezing her fingers in warning. She glanced up and he imperceptibly shook his head as he handed it over. Max's hands were like ice and she looked away, ignoring him.

"I want snug square knots around his hands and feet," instructed Marnie. "We don't want anything coming loose."

*Max, don't do it.*

MAX EMPTIED her mind, no longer thinking of what she was about to do. She could hear water rumbling over the rocks. It sounded much deeper than she'd initially thought. When Marnie began talking about the organophosphates, Max knew what had to be done and she didn't dare make eye contact with Zach.

He'd try to stop her. Max was the only one who could prevent this disaster from occurring now. As Marnie edged closer, Max took the rope and turned her back, bending over into her pack. She slid her hand into the top to retrieve her gun, moving her entire body around Zach while holding the rope so that it looked like she was tying him up. In reality she was transferring the Glock from her hand into Zach's waistband, out of Marnie's line of vision. Max finished her circuit around his body and looped the rope over his hands.

She wasn't doing a very good job; he'd be able to get himself loose. Marnie came nearer once Zach's hands appeared to be tied. The woman had been waiting for him to be immobilized before she approached them.

Max started on his feet, willing Marnie to get just a bit closer. She'd get only one chance at this, and Marnie's SIG-Sauer was bigger than her Glock.

Finally Marnie was at point-blank range. In one motion Max stood and pulled the gun out of Zach's waistband. This was different than shooting blindly into the rocks when they were going down into the cavern. But it all came back, like being on the firing range with Kirk.

Max fired three times. She was nervous. Two shots went wide, the sound reverberating against the walls of the cave.

The other must have hit its target, because Marnie looked up in surprise, blood blooming at her right leg. Her helmet light winked out just as Max saw the fat televisionlike remote hit the rocky floor along with the SIG.

Max dropped her Glock and dove for the remote detonator at the same time Marnie did. The light from Max's helmet broke as they both hit the ground and darkness descended like an impenetrable fog. Rocks dug into Max's back, but the adrenaline rush kept the impact from hurting like it normally would have. She got her fingers on the detonator and hung on.

Zach's carbide helmet light was the only illumination. Max and Marnie scuffled on the ground, rolling down the corridor toward the encroaching stream.

Max's foot connected with her pack and she heard rather than felt it fly through the air. She tried not to think about where her samples were ending up. She'd put them in a zippered plastic bag, hadn't she?

Then she and Marnie were rolling on the ground into the shallow rushing water and Max wasn't thinking anymore. She took a deep breath before icy water ran into her nose and mouth. It would get deeper the farther they rolled.

Marnie pulled her hair and grasped at the detonator. Max bit her hand. It was an all-out girl-fight in a subzero blender. Somehow they were standing again and Max got the detonator at the same time she heard the snick of a bullet being chambered.

Marnie had gotten her SIG back. Max felt the boreal steel of the barrel on the side of her temple. Glacial water rushed past their thighs, but somehow the barrel of that gun felt even colder. Pinpricks raced up Max's spine. This was it. She'd gambled and lost.

"Put the gun down, Marnie." Zach's voice thundered in the relative darkness.

"I can't miss from here," said Marnie, her breathing labored. Max remembered she'd been shot in the leg.

"Neither can I," said Zach. His voice was arctic, but it felt like a warm blanket to Max.

"Your girlfriend will die."

"If you get that detonator, she'll die anyway. Put the gun down." He chambered a round, as well.

Marnie gave a harsh laugh. Her back was to the corridor and the deeper, rapidly moving water. She was breathing harder and had pulled Max up against her. Max held tight to the detonator even when she felt the warmth of Marnie's body through her wet clothes.

"There's no way out of here on your own," said Zach. His voice was low and calm. "You need us to help you climb out."

Marnie's maniacal laughter echoed off the walls like the gunshots had earlier. "I was never supposed to get out that way."

In one motion she lifted the gun away from Max's head and fell backward into the swiftly moving water. She never came up for air. The deadly current simply carried her away into the darkest depths of the cave.

## Chapter Twenty-One

Initially, Zach heard only churning water. Then, in the single light of his helmet, he saw Max standing there, dripping wet and alone. Slowly she hobbled to his side. He'd gotten the ropes off his hands but not his feet. She knelt and untied him. Rising, she studied him with those blue, searching eyes.

"Thank you hardly seems sufficient," she said.

He cradled her to his chest. Would his heart rate ever return to normal? He couldn't believe how close he'd come to losing her.

"Don't worry." He smiled. "We'll come up with something."

"Is that a threat?" she asked.

"No, babe, that's a promise."

The gurgling noise ratcheted up a level. They turned to see what was causing the ominous sound. The rising flood had hit another passageway entrance and was being sucked down like an emptying sink drain. In the dim light it looked bizarre but had bought them some time.

"Do you think she's still alive?" Max asked.

Zach shook his head. "This water will go down for a while before it comes back up. Chances are she'll drown before she gets to a passage that has air pockets."

Max shuddered. "That's no less than she deserves, but what a hideous way to die."

He nodded. They finished untying his feet and walked back to the bacteria pond. He dug out a flashlight and an emergency headlight from his pack. "We've got to figure out what to do with that canister and how to get out of here."

"Will it fit in one of our packs?" asked Max.

"Maybe."

"And my samples? I kicked my pack somewhere when we were fighting."

Zach found her green pack submerged in the middle of the pool and didn't hesitate to wade in up to his chest.

"No, Zach. You'll contaminate the—"

He dove under the crystal-clear water and her voice became muffled. Breaking the surface, he made his way back to shore with the webbed strap clasped firmly in hand. Water lapped at his waist as tiny waves crashed against the rocky shoreline.

He walked out of the pond and handed Max her drowned pack, which was amazingly none the worse for wear. "The apocalypse is coming to this pool in less than an hour. I'm not going to hurt it."

She smiled sadly. "You're right." She'd stored her notebooks in a large zippered plastic bag along with the specimen jars, so all were intact.

It took some rearranging, but soon they were ready to go. The canister fit into Zach's pack once he'd taken out most of his supplies and transferred what would fit to Max's. The water from the corridor was within three feet of the pond when they were snugging shoulder straps to their backs.

Zach prepared their equipment. Ascenders and harnesses, everything clipped together and buckles tightened. They had to slug through frigid water to the exit corridor and the bottom of the fixed rope was floating when they got to their original entry point. Zach strapped Max in.

"Belay on," said Max.

"On belay," said Zach.

"Climb on." She grasped the rope between her hands.

"On climb."

Max started up the side of the rock face.

"Be careful," warned Zach. "Your feet are wet and aren't going to grip as well."

"Right."

She went up about ten feet while Zach stood in the water holding the line. It was cold. Freezing. Like shots of pins and needles to the ankles and calves.

He hoped she scaled the wall fast. He didn't relish a free climb with numb feet. Normally he'd set some protection above the water line and clamp in until Max reached the top, but she needed someone on belay.

As it was, she was having problems holding on to the rock. Most likely her hands were numb. Getting a handhold had to be difficult.

She stopped climbing and hung on a moment.

"Max, what's going on?"

"Cramping. In my calves and my fingers. They're freezing. I'm scared I'm going to fall."

"I know you're cold." Zach's own teeth were starting to chatter. "But you're not going to fall. I've got you roped in and I'll be able to catch you if you slip. But you do need to stop and rest for a minute. Get those hands warmed up. Above your head about three feet there's a ledge. We passed it on the way down. It's nice and deep." It was practically a mini cave. "I want you to head for that. Crawl in and take a break."

"What about you?"

Below him the water was rising. "I'm fine. I'll be right there. I'm coming up as soon as you get onto the ledge." He held his hands up to his helmet, the heat from the lamp warming his hands slightly.

Something strange was happening. The water was coming in at a much faster rate than before. It would be to his thighs in a matter of minutes. They had to get to the top of this fissure and back on the trail before their path was blocked by flooding.

Max climbed to the ledge. Zach was relieved to see her feet disappear over the edge.

"Okay, Max. Unclip your harness from the line. But no getting crazy on the rim of the ledge, okay?"

"You're funny."

"I try."

He was just putting his hands on the rock to start his ascent when she screamed. Her pack plummeted toward him and Zach flattened himself against the wall. The pack landed with a thunderous splat in the water only to be whisked away in the current and slammed against a large rock in the middle of the corridor. But he didn't look to see if it stayed there. He was immediately looking up. In his mind's eye he saw Max tumbling toward him.

He shook the vision from his head. "Are you okay?" he shouted. He could hear the panic in his voice.

"Yes, I just… I'm an idiot. I tripped. I'm sorry. Where's the pack? Can I come back down there?"

"Hell no. You stay there or I'll drown you myself." Zach's heart rate was skyrocketing into the stratosphere and his voice was sharper than he'd intended.

He exhaled and looked around for the pack, knowing they weren't going anywhere without those samples. He looked to the rock. No surprise, the pack wasn't there anymore, but it could have sunk right beside it.

Water flowed around his waist, but didn't seem to be moving as quickly as before. Probably because it was so much deeper. But God, it was so damn cold. He hoped to hell Max's pack hadn't gone off down one of the new lower offshoots that was a few yards away. The water there was like a flushing toilet, sucking down deep into the depths of the cave. If the pack reached that point, he'd never get it back.

"Max, you've got to pull my pack out of here before I can go look for yours. I can't risk this canister getting wet." *Or my drowning down here with it strapped to my back.* Of course, there was no need to mention that part.

"Oh." There was a moment of silence as he was slipping his pack off and clipping it to the rope. "I understand." He got the distinct impression she understood completely.

He double-clipped the pack to the rope. His only way out. She pulled the pack and its deadly cargo up toward her ledge. As soon as the canister left his hands, he started walking toward the rock where he'd last seen Max's pack. He'd kept the waterproof flashlight, hoping the combination of his helmet light and the flash would help him find it.

Rushing water cast eerie shadows and lots of reflection, but no fluorescent-green nylon pack. The water was now to his chest and like being in a freezer. He felt all around the huge boulder, hoping the pack had sunk and wedged beside it.

He couldn't reach to the floor of the corridor without putting his head under the gently undulating waves. The top of the rock was flat with a slight indentation in the center. He took off his safety helmet and placed it there. Taking a deep breath, he went under the icy current with his flashlight. Frigid water stung his eyes. He felt along one side of the stone— hoping, praying for a webbed backpack strap.

Nothing.

He came up gasping for air and moved to the next side of the rock face. He was treading slowly, still his foot caught on something, almost pulling him under. He took a deep breath to check it out.

It wasn't the pack, only another large rock. He was going to have to swim to keep from hurting himself on hidden ob-stacles. This was taking too long. He pushed away thoughts of hypothermia and got to the other side of the boulder. He took one more breath before going under.

There, a miracle. The pack was jammed between two rocks next to the large boulder. He went under three times before he could shift it loose.

"I've got it," he gasped. He realized his voice wasn't very loud. The cold was getting to him. That thought alone spurred him on.

He grabbed his helmet. The water was to his neck and he couldn't feel his hands by the time he got to the wall. Max was peering over the rim of the ledge. He could see her tiny emergency headlamp winking at him through the darkness.

How was he going to climb with numb hands? He looked into the inky blackness of the water swirling around him. There wasn't any choice.

"Max, send the rope back down!" He wrapped his fingers around his helmet, trying to warm them on the lantern's heat source before he had to climb. He repeated the same procedure with her pack that he'd done with his own, making sure to add the flashlight when he remembered Max's claustrophobic fear of the dark. He was thinking positive about making it out, but all the same he didn't want any extra weight on his back. "Okay, pull it up." He put his hands on the rock.

"Wait." Max's head appeared at the ledge again. "Are you free soloing?"

Technically, that's not what it was. He was using equipment. He shrugged, although she couldn't see him in the dim light and deep water. "It's the only way to get to you."

He took a leash and set some protection as far above his head as he could manage from the ground. He had to get out of the current and get the blood flow back into his own feet before he could begin the real ascent. He pulled himself up and strapped in, out of the icy flood at last. He hung there as long as he dared, slapping his palms together, then began the longest climb of his life.

One hand over the other, that's all he had to do. Just keep going until he was there. This was supposed to be easy; it's what he loved to do. But his feet were wet and his fingers were numb. He was breaking every rule he'd ever set for himself about safety. But Max was waiting for him. There were no other options.

# Chapter Twenty-Two

Fifteen agonizing minutes later Zach reached the ledge and Max pulled him over the rim. He landed in the middle of her. Too wiped out to care that this was very uncool, he didn't move for five minutes. He just lay there, breathing hard, grateful she was soft.

"Don't you ever, ever do that again," she said.

He realized he was crushing her and struggled to roll to the side, too spent to sit up.

She got in his face. "That wasn't what I meant."

Confused, he raised an eyebrow, not even sure he wanted to know what she meant.

"Well, climbing that wall won't make my top ten." He raised his head and looked around at the small space. "This is almost cozy."

He pulled back and rubbed his numb hands together, struggling to get the feeling back in them. She took his fingers and rubbed them between hers.

"Don't you joke about this. Not right now. I—" Her voice broke and he saw the tear streaks on her muddy face. "I don't know what I would have done—"

He remembered her claustrophobia and paralyzing fear of the dark and wanted to kick himself back down the wall he'd just scaled. She must have been freaking out up here while he made that climb.

"You'd have made it out." He pulled his hands away to reach for her, but she batted him back.

"That's not what I meant, either. I don't know what I'd have done without you. I don't want to know what I'd do without…you."

He looked at her, not sure he was quite understanding. But he wanted to believe her; he was desperate to believe her.

"I watched you climbing that wall and realized I couldn't control it. The outcome. What happened to you. It physically hurt me to see you risking your life, even though it was the only way out. My only way out. I want the chance to let go and see what happens to us without my trying to control it all or put it in a box. Please let me have that chance." Her tears were falling in earnest now and she'd taken his hands again to rub them between hers.

He studied her a moment in stunned silence, not sure how to respond to what he was hearing. He wanted to hold her. Instead, he reached up to gently wipe her tears with his fingertips. His hands were torn up, a mess from the climb, but it was all he knew to do in the face of her emotions.

"I think that can be arranged." He kept his voice low, trying to soothe her. This was what he wanted. He just couldn't quite believe he might actually get it. He couldn't believe Max really wanted him.

Then she was in his arms, weeping. This was not what he'd pictured, either, but he'd take Max any way he could get her—even in tears.

He held her and kissed the top of her head. "It'll be all right, you'll see. We have time to figure this out. We do. But first, we have to climb out of here."

Those words cut off the flow of tears. She met his gaze. "How exactly? I can't do a free solo climb."

"I know that. You're going to be roped in with protection. It's a bit different from climbing on straight belay, but you'll be fine."

She gave him a highly skeptical look but pulled herself together and nodded. "Okay."

He went ahead of her and set some extra clamps in addition to the ones from their journey down the wall. When he came back to the ledge, he triple-checked her harness.

"You're going to clip in and go up just like before and you're going to be fine. I'm right behind you. I'm not going to let anything happen to you."

She smiled bravely. "I'm counting on that."

TEN HARROWING minutes later, they reached the peak of the fissure. Max's head was pounding and she never wanted to climb onto anything higher than the escalator at Macy's for the rest of her life. But they were finally at the top and making their way back to the original path.

She followed Zach along the uneven trail, at times crouching down and hunching over when the ceiling became too low for their height. As they crossed the natural bridge where Tim had fallen, a cold ball of dread had her tensing up in the middle of the pathway. Far below, water gurgled in the depths of the cavern. When they'd made it all the way across the moss-covered stone, she could breathe again.

Zach was quiet, even when they stopped to eat Clif bars and drink water. The waterfall chamber where they'd left Kirk and the others was deserted. Apparently Harris had come back and gotten them out.

According to her watch, it was five-thirty in the morning. They'd been in Devil's Hollow for seven hours.

Zach took off his pack in preparation for crawling through the tube into the vertical entry chamber. He stopped to pick up a discarded bandage. "Almost there." He seemed reluctant to take the final leg of the journey.

"So what are you going to do now?" he asked. "You have your samples. I suppose you'll be going home?"

"I'm not sure." A tremor of uncertainty ran down her spine. *Hadn't they talked about this on the ledge?* She thought they'd come to some kind of understanding.

"I imagine you've got some kind of bulletproof plan?" he asked.

*No. I thought you understood.* Max stopped in the middle of the path to peer at him through the darkness. It was now or never. "I suppose a lot of that depends on you."

Zach stopped, too. "I don't understand."

"Did you not hear me back there?" She pointed over her shoulder the way they'd come.

He didn't answer, so she kept talking, worried she'd lose her nerve if he interrupted.

"What part of 'I don't want to control this' did you miss?" He looked at her then and she didn't miss his eyes arrowing into hers, even in the dim glow of her headlamp. She couldn't make out exactly what his expression was, but it wasn't disbelief.

"I want to make sure you understand me, Zach. Because I really do trust you and I want to be with you, and it scares me to death. So much so that I'll quit Earth Pharm as soon as we walk out of here if you promise me not to risk your life like that again."

She didn't pause for breath. Zach's face was completely blank; she had no idea what he was thinking. "Don't talk to me about plans. 'Cause I have no idea what the hell I'm doi—"

He was kissing her before she finished. One moment he'd been staring at her with a completely inscrutable look and the next he had her wrapped in his arms, raising a blistering heat that made her forget everything except how much she wanted this to work.

"I'd never ask you to give up your research," he whispered between kisses.

"We're not going to be easy," she murmured, coming up for air.

He laughed and she could feel the vibration of it deep in her own chest. "Hell, no. I think we're going to be a street rumble. And my ego will no doubt be beaten and bloodied a time or two along the way."

She wanted to deny that but realized she couldn't. "And you really want this?"

"I said my ego, Max, not my heart. I believe you're worth the risk."

An idea so new to her, it was unfathomable. Letting someone in. Both frightening and exhilarating at the same time.

"You're sure?" she asked. *You want me?*

He didn't answer right away. Instead, he regarded her with the same intensity that had been so disconcerting just two days ago. This was a whole new beginning. With so much promise on so many levels. The ultimate exercise in letting go.

He nodded and those *GQ* dimples appeared. "Oh yeah, I'm sure."

\* \* \* \* \*

*Celebrate 60 years of pure reading pleasure
with Harlequin®!*

*Step back in time and enjoy a sneak preview of an exciting
anthology from Harlequin® Historical with*
*THE DIAMONDS OF WELBOURNE MANOR*

This compelling anthology features three stories about
the outrageous Fitzmanning sisters. Meet Annalise, who
is never at a loss for words… But that can change with
an unexpected encounter in the forest.

*Available May 2009 from Harlequin® Historical.*

"I'm the illegitimate daughter of notoriously scandalous parents, Mr. Milford. Candidates for my hand are unlikely to be lining up at the gates."

"Don't be so quick to discount your charms, my dear. Or the charm of your substantial dowry. Or even your brothers' influence. There are as many reasons to marry as there are marriages."

Annalise snorted. "Oh, yes. Perhaps I shall marry for dynastic reasons, or perhaps for property or influence. After all, a loveless, practical marriage worked out so well for my mother."

"Well, you've routed me on that one. I can think of no suitable rejoinder." Ned rose to his feet and extended his hand. "And since that is the case, let me be the first to wish you a long and happy spinsterhood."

Her mouth gaped open. And then she laughed.

And he froze.

This was the first time, Ned realized. The first time he'd seen her eyes light up and her mouth curl. The first time he'd witnessed her features melded together in glorious accord to produce exquisite beauty.

Unbelievable what a change came over her face. Unheard of what effect her throaty, rasping laughter had on his body. It pounded a beat upon his ear, quickly taken up by his pulse. It echoed through him, finally residing in his stirring nether regions.

So easily she did it, awakened these sensations within him—without any apparent effort at all. And she had called him potentially dangerous? Clearly the intelligent thing for him to do would be to steer clear, to leave her to the tender ministrations of Lord Peter Blackthorne.

"You were right." She smiled up at him as she took his hand and climbed to her feet. "I do feel better."

Ah, well. When had he ever chosen the intelligent path?

He did not relinquish her hand. He used it to pull her in, close enough that he could feel the warmth of her. "At the risk of repeating Lord Peter's mistake and anticipating too much— may I ask if you'll be my partner in battledore tomorrow?"

Her smiled dimmed. Her breath came a little faster. His own had gone shallow, as if he'd just run a race—and lost. He ran his gaze over the appealing lift of her brow and the curious angle of her chin. His index finger twitched.

"I should like that," she said.

His finger trembled again and he lifted it, traced the pink and tender shell of her ear, the unique sweep of her jaw. Her pulse leaped beneath her skin, triggering his own. Slowly he tilted her chin up, waiting for her to object, to step back, to slap his hand away.

She did none of those eminently sensible things. Which left him free to do the entirely impractical thing.

Baby soft, the skin of her lips. Her whole body trembled when he touched her there.

He leaned in. Her eyes closed, even as she stood straight against him, strung as tight as a bow. He pressed his mouth to hers. It was a soft kiss, sweet and chaste. And yet he was hot and hard and as ready as he'd ever been in his life.

She drew back a little. Sighed. Their breath mingled a moment before she slowly backed away.

"Oh," she breathed. Her dark eyes were full of wonder and

something that looked like fear. He took a step toward her, but she only shook her head. His outstretched hand fell to his side as she turned to disappear into the wood. This was the first time, Ned realized. The first time, since he'd come to the house party at Welbourne Manor, that he'd seen her eyes light up.

\* \* \* \* \*

*Follow Ned and Annalise's story in May 2009 in*
*THE DIAMONDS OF WELBOURNE MANOR.*
*Available May 2009 from Harlequin® Historical.*

*Available in the series romance section,*
*or in the historical romance section,*
*wherever books are sold.*

We'll be spotlighting a different series every month
throughout 2009 to celebrate our 60th anniversary.

### Look for Harlequin®
### American Romance® in June!

Join us for a year-long celebration of the rugged
American male! From cops to cowboys—
Men Made in America has the hero
you've been dreaming about!

Look for

# The Chief Ranger

### by Rebecca Winters, on sale in June!

# Do you crave dark and sensual paranormal tales?

## Get your fix with Silhouette Nocturne!

---

### In print:
Two new titles available every month
wherever books are sold.

### Online:
Nocturne eBooks available monthly
from **www.silhouettenocturne.com**.

### Nocturne Bites:
Short sensual paranormal stories
available monthly online from
**www.nocturnebites.com** and in print
with the Nocturne Bites collections
available April 2009 and October 2009
wherever books are sold.

---

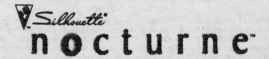

**www.silhouettenocturne.com**
**www.paranormalromanceblog.com**

# REQUEST YOUR FREE BOOKS!

## 2 FREE NOVELS PLUS 2 FREE GIFTS!

**HARLEQUIN®**

# INTRIGUE®

## Breathtaking Romantic Suspense

**YES!** Please send me 2 FREE Harlequin Intrigue® novels and my 2 FREE gifts (gifts are worth about $10). After receiving them, if I don't wish to receive any more books, I can return the shipping statement marked "cancel." If I don't cancel, I will receive 6 brand-new novels every month and be billed just $4.24 per book in the U.S. or $4.99 per book in Canada. That's a savings of close to 15% off the cover price! It's quite a bargain! Shipping and handling is just 25¢ per book*. I understand that accepting the 2 free books and gifts places me under no obligation to buy anything. I can always return a shipment and cancel at any time. Even if I never buy another book from Harlequin, the two free books and gifts are mine to keep forever.

182 HDN EEZ7    382 HDN EEZK

| | | |
|---|---|---|
| Name | (PLEASE PRINT) | |
| Address | | Apt. # |
| City | State/Prov. | Zip/Postal Code |

Signature (if under 18, a parent or guardian must sign)

### Mail to the **Harlequin Reader Service:**
**IN U.S.A.:** P.O. Box 1867, Buffalo, NY 14240-1867
**IN CANADA:** P.O. Box 609, Fort Erie, Ontario L2A 5X3

Not valid to current subscribers of Harlequin Intrigue books.

**Are you a current subscriber of Harlequin Intrigue books
and want to receive the larger-print edition?
Call 1-800-873-8635 today!**

* Terms and prices subject to change without notice. Prices do not include applicable taxes. Sales tax applicable in N.Y. Canadian residents will be charged applicable provincial taxes and GST. Offer not valid in Quebec. This offer is limited to one order per household. All orders subject to approval. Credit or debit balances in a customer's account(s) may be offset by any other outstanding balance owed by or to the customer. Please allow 4 to 6 weeks for delivery. Offer available while quantities last.

**Your Privacy:** Harlequin is committed to protecting your privacy. Our Privacy Policy is available online at www.eHarlequin.com or upon request from the Reader Service. From time to time we make our lists of customers available to reputable third parties who may have a product or service of interest to you. If you would prefer we not share your name and address, please check here. ☐

HI09

# You're invited to join our Tell Harlequin Reader Panel!

By joining our new reader panel you will:

- Receive Harlequin® books—they are FREE and yours to keep with no obligation to purchase anything!
- Participate in fun online surveys
- Exchange opinions and ideas with women just like you
- Have a say in our new book ideas and help us publish the best in women's fiction

*In addition, you will have a chance to win great prizes and receive special gifts!*
*See Web site for details. Some conditions apply.*
*Space is limited.*

## To join, visit us at
# www.TellHarlequin.com.

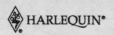
# INTRIGUE

## COMING NEXT MONTH

### Available May 12, 2009

#### #1131 HUNTING DOWN THE HORSEMAN by B.J. Daniels
*Whitehorse, Montana: The Corbetts*
A stuntman who has never given a thought to marriage reconsiders when an adventurous trick rider catches his eye. When a set of incidents on their movie location puts her life in danger, he is determined to catch the culprit...and to get the girl.

#### #1132 COLLECTING EVIDENCE by Rita Herron
*Kenner County Crime Unit*
To her, the sexy FBI agent is a perfect stranger. Amnesia has wiped away her memories of their affair...and the crime she witnessed. As her memories return, he must protect her—and the son who may be his—from a killer.

#### #1133 PRICELESS NEWBORN PRINCE by Ann Voss Peterson
*Diamonds and Daddies*
Rebels have forcefully overthrown his rule, but when the woman he loves and his newborn son are threatened, the prince must make a choice: fight for his family or the future of his country?

#### #1134 INTERROGATING THE BRIDE by Carla Cassidy
*The Recovery Men*
Repossessing a plane is an easy assignment for the former navy SEAL, but the vivacious stowaway in a wedding dress proves to be a problem. Someone is framing her for murder, and he is the only one who can help clear her name.

#### #1135 KISSING THE KEY WITNESS by Jenna Ryan
When dangerous information about a powerful crime boss falls into the unsuspecting hands of an E.R. doctor, it is a homicide lieutenant who is on call to save her life.

#### #1136 SAVED BY THE MONARCH by Dana Marton
*Defending the Crown*
A prince is betrothed to a free-spirited American who wants nothing to do with an arranged marriage. When they are kidnapped, the prince must fight not only for their survival, but also for the heart of the woman he never expected to love.

HICNMBPA0409

www.eHarlequin.com